THE BLIND IMPRESS

For Keith Ridler and Judith Loveridge
and for Les and Mary Cleveland.

THE BLIND IMPRESS

MICHAEL JACKSON

The Dunmore Press

©1997 Michael Jackson
©1997 The Dunmore Press Ltd

First Published in 1997
by
The Dunmore Press Ltd
P.O. Box 5115
Palmerston North
New Zealand

Australian Supplier:
Federation Press
P.O. Box 45
Annandale 2038 NSW
Australia
Ph: (02) 9552-2200
Fax: (02) 9552-1681

ISBN 0 86469 307 9

Text: Caslon540 BT 10.5/14.5
Printer: The Dunmore Printing Company Ltd
                Palmerston North
Cover design: Katherine McGougan
                Michael Jackson

Copyright. No part of this book may be reproduced without written permission except in the case of brief quotations embodied in critical articles and reviews.

And once you have walked the length of your mind, what
You command is clear as a lading-list.
Anything else must not, for you, be thought
    To exist.

And what's the profit? Only that, in time,
We half identify the blind impress
All our behavings bear, may trace it home.
    But to confess,

On that green evening when our death begins,
Just what it was, is hardly satisfying,
Since it applied only to one man once,
    And that one dying.

        (Philip Larkin, from *Continuing to Live*)

The Blind Impress

Contents

I

1. That Green Evening — 11
2. The Blind Impress — 15
3. The Other Side of the Tracks — 27
4. Of the Woe that is in Marriage — 36
5. Manawatu — 45
6. Fires of No Return — 49
7. Fugue — 63
8. Shots in the Dark — 68
9. Recaptured — 77
10. No Quarter — 84
11. Escape — 99

II

12. Starting Over — 107
13. Beyond the Call of Duty — 115
14. Talking to Jack Hansen — 121
15. Passing Strange — 136
16. Still Life with Lading Lists — 143

III

17.	The Remaining Pieces	153
18.	Guilt and Shame	162
19.	Death's Secretary	175
20.	Stories Happen	182

Acknowledgements   191

Notes   193

I

The Blind Impress

1

That Green Evening

He is sitting outside his garden shed. A panama hat shades his face. Rakes and hoes are propped against the wall; seed potatoes are spread out on superphosphate sacks. He lights his briar and tosses the match away.

I was three when my grandfather retired from the police. He began telling me stories before I even understood what stories were.

'My, the living,' (Yorkshire accent, rueful shake of the head) 'to look at him you wouldn't think he could make anything but a nuisance of himself.'

He pauses. Holds his pipe away from his face. Wipes a film of spittle from his lips with the back of his hand. The cabbage patch is spattered with white butterflies.

'Aye, there wasn't only one thing 'e could do, could that lad, and that was make a public nuisance of himself.'

My grandfather seems to brood for a moment on the failings and foibles of men, and I can smell blood and bone and hear the river stumbling through the bush ....

In the years my grandfather is remembering, Saturday was late-night shopping. Farmers drove in from the back blocks and stood along the footpath, backs to the street, smoking cigarettes and complaining about the falling price of wool. Wives went shopping.

A lot of town boys resented the young farmers. Would get drunk and pick fights. One bloke in particular was an inveterate trouble-maker. My grandfather was 'forever being called out to deal with him'. But telling this story, my grandfather doesn't mention the misdemeanour. It's the young man's pride which is at stake, not his guilt. When my grandfather arrests him outside the post office, he avoids taking him directly to the police station because this will mean going along the thronged main street. Instead, he takes an alleyway into a back street so the miscreant will not be seen and shamed.

In 1960 when my grandfather died, I went back to Moabite for the funeral. After a Methodist service, the cortège set off for the cemetery. As our car turned after the hearse toward the cemetery gates, I noticed a group of old men standing on the opposite side of the road, heads bowed, hats in their hands. One was the man whose public humiliation my grandfather averted fifty years ago.

My uncles inherited my grandfather's fob watch, watch chain, and police baton. My legacy has been my grandfather's stories.

One story in particular he returned to time and time again. It was also a story about youth, and loss, and guilt and shame.

In 1910 a young man called Joe Pawelka was arrested in the Manawatu and remanded on charges of housebreaking, arson and theft. His escape from police custody triggered the most intense manhunt in New Zealand since the military pursuit in the late 1860s of the Maori resistance leader Te Kooti. During the weeks that Pawelka was on the run, two men were shot dead, buildings were set on fire, shops and homes burgled, and panic engulfed a province. My grandfather was stationed in Levin at the time and was among police reinforcements brought to the Manawatu for the manhunt. Like many New Zealanders, he would remember 'The Powelka Campaign' as the biggest news story of the year, with banner headlines fuelling the general 'hysteria' and 'pandemonium'. 'Mad Orgy of Manslaying', *Truth* declared. 'Wild Rumour and False Alarm.'

Recaptured and brought to trial, Joe Pawelka got twenty-one years hard labour for breaking and entering, theft, arson and escape. Many people, including my grandfather, thought the sentence vengeful and unjust, and on the wintry August day in 1911 when Pawelka escaped from the Terrace Gaol in Wellington, never to be heard of again, my grandfather was happy to conclude that poetic justice had been done.

Stories have a habit of generating stories. They come to nest, one inside the other, like Chinese boxes, each a window onto another's world. This is what happened to my grandfather's story about Joe Pawelka.

In 1973, after several years abroad, I came back to New Zealand with my wife and daughter and went to live in the Manawatu. Some of the places where Joe Pawelka had lived, worked and taken refuge became as familiar to me as they had been for him, and three years later, when I published my first book of poems, *Latitudes of Exile*, I alluded to some of the connections that were beginning to take hold in my imagination ....

> This poem has been written before;
> it has been written by men and women
> who never read a line of poetry all their lives;
> it has been said and imagined many times;
> it is the poem of the labyrinth,
> of the other way, of forgotten roads
> and of the wheel of chance

and today, travelling the Pahiatua Track
to Scarborough, I think of Joe Pawelka
and what went wrong for him,
my grandfather's story of a hunted man
who vanished from the cells
in which he was condemned
for burning down a school,
housebreaking and escape,
for bothering his wife when a magistrate
ordered their separation,
who scrawled a note with the lead of a bullet
and signed it 'a man against the world'.

Like my grandfather, I always wanted to know what went wrong for Joe Pawelka and what became of him. But this is not simply a question of what happened after he escaped and disappeared. More compellingly, it is a matter of the transformations his persona and story have undergone, of the way they have entered the diffuse and dimly lit world of our collective imagination, blurring with countless other stories, pub yarns and anecdotes until they resemble a kind of national self-portrait on which we work tirelessly, unselfconsciously and without much sense of the finished picture.

This is why my search for Joe Pawelka came to encompass many lives, including my own, and why this book is also a story about stories: an allegory of events that outstrip the life of Joe Pawelka, bridging the known and the imagined, negotiating that open ground where the shadows of the past define the fugitive shape of our future.

CB8O

2

The
Blind Impress

My plane came into Wellington over the strait, buffeted by high winds. I peered out at raw-boned hills, the sea like saliva, black rocks strewn with driftwood.

Leaving Immigration and Customs, I almost collided with a middle-aged couple who were waiting for someone off my flight. The woman was holding up a placard with a balloon attached to it: *Welcome Home Nigel!* They looked anxious. Then I realised that Nigel was directly behind me. 'Hi Mum,' he said, without emotion.

'Hi,' she said. 'Do you like it?'

'Yeah, it's good,' he said.

They were talking about the sign and the balloon. There were no embraces. No more words. The father grunted and looked away, as if embarrassed to be seen performing such an intimate rite in such a public place.

For a moment I was unsure which way to go. I stood in the middle of the concourse, trying to spot a bus/taxi sign. There was a young man standing next to me, also looking up and down the concourse. He had cropped, peroxided hair, silver earrings, a black designer leather jacket, slim-fit black cords, and hand-tooled black leather boots. When he saw his friend, he waved. 'Harry!' The two men embraced, heads buried in each other's necks, eyes closed. Real tears.

Driving into the city, I remembered how empty my homeland could be. So little outward sign of neighbourhood. Colin McCahon's 'landscape with too few lovers'. Was it Robert Morley who said he once visited New Zealand but it was closed?

Next morning the wind was coming off the sea, and the sky bruised. Between rain squalls, a marine light flooded the glass facades of the downtown office buildings. Over breakfast in an espresso bar, I read the morning paper. The first black vote in the South African elections had been cast in Wellington, where Nomoza Paintin – an imposter, it later turned out – lived in political exile. She called the moment euphoric. 'I felt in the presence of my ancestors today,' she said. 'I felt I was voting for them.'

I remembered the cold, rainswept streets where we marched in 1981, chanting the ANC slogan *Amandla Ngawethu* against the Springbok tour. And as I made my way downtown to the National Library, my thoughts went back to the street clashes, the cries of 'Shame', the divided families and troubled friendships that had brought so many New Zealanders to the realisation that violence was closer to home than they'd ever imagined. For all our pacific imagery, egalitarian myths and talk of racial tolerance, our country had suddenly revealed itself to be a place of unhealed wounds and entrenched inequality. In the ashen landscapes of the central North Island, long-dormant volcanoes were erupting. But the violence was also in our houses and our hearts. We saw it in the faces of abused children and battered wives. We nurtured it in the anxious hope that our children would see no evil, hear no evil, speak no evil, and feel no evil. And we created it in the poverty and powerlessness that drove many down the road of violence as the only road that would give them room to manoeuvre and confirm their worth.

Was New Zealand an accident waiting to happen? Had we kept ourselves too long in the dark about the passions and quandaries that governed us? In coming to terms with our history, could we make peace with ourselves?

At the National Library, photocopying pages of the Wellington and Manawatu newspapers that carried the Pawelka story in 1910, I had no idea whether my journey back in time would provide any answers to these questions. But I held out the hope that in returning to one place where the questions had been raised, I might better understand the long shadows they had cast in our lives.

Joe Pawelka's grandfather, Ferdinand Pavelka, emigrated to New Zealand in 1873. He'd been a glazier in Stramberk, Moravia – a crownland east of Bohemia in the Austro-Hungarian empire. A year after reaching New Zealand, Ferdinand sent for his wife, Rosina, and their five children. Rosina, then forty-three, would forever remember dipping her fingers in the Danube on the day they left.

The Pavelkas settled near Oxford, North Canterbury, where there was work building roads, and felling and milling timber. In 1885, Ferdinand's second son, Jozef, married Louise König who had, coincidentally, come out from Moravia with her family on the *Stonehouse* – the same ship which brought Jozef's family to New Zealand.*

Joseph's mother, Rosina, disapproved of Louisa, and tried to prevent the marriage. In this close-knit Catholic family, the matriarch had the right to decree who belonged and who did not. Respect for her authority was practically synonymous with respect for God; she was the family's fountainhead of power and moral arbiter. It was a grave matter for a son to go against his mother's wishes, and when

---

* The names get Anglicised in New Zealand: Jozef becomes Joseph; Alois becomes Louise, then Louisa; König becomes Koenig or King. Pawelka (or Pavelka) is the Czech diminutive of Paul (Pavel). In 1910, newspapers regularly misspelled the name Powelka.

Joseph married Louisa without his mother's blessing, the fifty-seven-year-old matriarch construed it, in part, as a violation of their faith. When Louisa's first child, Mary Rosina, died two months after she was born, Rosina declared the death to be a divine judgement on the ill-advised marriage.

John Joseph Thomas (Joe) Pawelka began life in the shadow of this loss. One wonders what passed through Rosina's mind when he was born on the first of August 1887, sixteen months after Mary Rosina's death. Did she consider him doomed as well? And when Joe's life took its tragic turn, did she conclude that he, who showed no more regard for God than his father had, was also divinely cursed?**

In 1891, when Joe was four and his sister Agnes two, the family left North Canterbury and followed Joe's maverick Uncle John to the North Island where he had opened a butcher's shop in a bush settlement called Kimbolton. The break cannot have been easy. Among the Moravian migrants, kinship was the wellspring of a person's security and identity. It was also one's tie to the past. In choosing autonomy over these blood ties, Joseph was repudiating his mother's old-world domination and nostalgia, breaking away from the suffocating insularity of the immigrant community, and distancing himself from the Moravian church to which he had, in any event, never been devoutly attached. By marrying Louisa when he was twenty-four, he had begun an irrevocable process of estrangement from Rosina. Now aged thirty-one, he marked the finality of the separation by changing the spelling of his name from Pavelka to Pawelka.

Kimbolton stands on a windblown ridge above the Oroua River. When the Pawelkas travelled up the newly metalled road from

---

**   The redoubtable Rosina died in her 84th year (1913), a year-and-a-half after Joe's disappearance.

Feilding in 1891, they would have looked out over a devastated landscape of surveyors' tracks, dead trees, splintered logs, stumps, slab whares and scorched earth. A country stunned into silence. No motors. Few forest birds. A dog barking in the distance. The bellowing of a bull.

Ranged along one side of Kimbolton's main street were a hotel, two stores, a post office, blacksmith's shop, library, public hall, stockyard and school. Opposite was a wasteland of stumps and scrub.

The land, at £1 an acre, was being broken in. Intractable forests of totara, hinau and rimu were felled and fired. Grass was sown among the ruins. Fences defined properties. Roads enclosed blocks.

But the broken land played havoc with those who claimed it. The Oroua shingled-up and flooded with run-off from autumn rains. In winter, bush tracks became quagmires, impassable even to bullock teams and horses. In summer, smoke from bush fires blotted out the sun, and dry winds stripped the topsoil from tenuous farms. In January 1898, one fire, fanned by gale-force winds from the west, razed a dozen Kimbolton homes and several shops before sweeping down into the Oroua valley and the ranges beyond. The acrid smoke blinded people for days. What impression this left in the mind of eleven-year-old Joe Pawelka one can only guess.

It is also hard to know exactly how immigrants from central Europe fared in this predominantly Anglo settlement. The Pawelkas' North Canterbury life had been ruled by bonds of kinship and the Catholic community. In Kimbolton, a Wesleyan church was built in 1891 (the year the Pawelkas arrived), but until 1912 there was no Catholic church, and a priest had to travel up from Feilding to say mass in Catholic homes. One old-timer, who had lived in Kimbolton since 1911, told me that the Catholic–Protestant division surfaced only on Sundays and during life crises:

> The thing that used to amaze me was that people could go out and work together from Monday to Saturday night, but at midnight on Saturday the bloody blinds came down. And the same thing applied in the blimmin' cemetery. The Catholic part of the cemetery, the Protestant part of the cemetery, somebody else's part of the cemetery ...!

Another younger informant, whose uncle was Protestant, remembered being told that Joe Pawelka's evasion of the law during the manhunt was 'a Catholic conspiracy'.

Most Kimbolton shops were owned by English, Irish or Scottish settlers. Already engrained was the New Zealand habit of joining clubs and forming committees as a way of defeating loneliness and creating some sense of social solidarity. But those who belonged to the cricket club, tennis club, football club, farmers' club, rifle club, and debating society, or were members of the school committee, coronation committee, concert party and flag committee were seldom foreign or Maori. The very names of the settlement –

Birmingham first, then Kimbolton – memorialised connections with England. In 1897 Queen Victoria's Diamond Jubilee was celebrated enthusiastically and local men enlisted to fight for Queen and Empire in the Boer War, convinced that the future of their colony was inextricably tied up with the motherland.

Joseph Pawelka worked as a grave-digger and casual labourer. In those years, grass harvesting was a major export industry. Every summer, cocksfoot, fescue, blue grass and rye seed was harvested from the newly-cleared land. Gangs of men with sickles moved across the stumpy paddocks, gathering sheaves and stooking them to dry. They threshed the grass with wooden flails on canvas sheets, then lifted the canvas into the wind to winnow the chaff from the grain.

When Joe Pawelka left school in 1900 at age thirteen, he worked for a while with his father collecting seed, and then, at his mother's urging, he apprenticed himself to his Uncle John. But John Pawelka had left Kimbolton by this time, and if Joe did learn butchery from his uncle, it must have been elsewhere.

At the height of the manhunt in 1910, a *New Zealand Times* reporter went up to Kimbolton to interview people about the fugitive. 'Everybody I spoke to in Kimbolton seemed heartily sorry for Powelka,' the reporter wrote, 'and all with whom he had dealings say that Powelka was a thoroughly upright fellow, who could be trusted with anything.'

The reporter learned that Joe had attended the local school and been considered 'a very smart boy' by his master, though he quit after Standard 7. References were also made to Joe's 'very passionate' nature: 'Even when a very small boy, his morose moods were a subject of comment.'

In due course there would be talk, not of mood swings or a 'bad temper', but of a 'lunatic' with a 'deranged mind', given to 'mad fits'. Are passion and madness always too close for comfort? Can the good citizen only construe disregard for the law as evidence of some psychological aberration? If something goes wrong in a person's life, must we always look for some pathology in early childhood?

One story has it that Joe didn't get on with his father – that his father had a quick temper, too. 'Old Joe, he had a terrific temper. It was passed on to young Joe. Joe got it from his father. Old Joe used to beat all the kids except the youngest, Helen. Agnes got plenty of hidings as a kid. Belted around the bum. And he was pretty nasty toward his wife at times. Though he was never aggressive in public ....'

According to this story, the ill-feeling between father and son was 'the reason Joe cleared out'. Joseph may have been jealous of the intense bond between Louise and Joe, and one is tempted to see Joe as someone too much indulged by his mother, so that he grows intolerant of being crossed, harbours some smouldering resentment when he is forced out into the world at thirteen to fend for himself.

Here is a photo of Joe with his sister Agnes and brother Jack in 1903. They are outdoors, probably in the garden behind their house in Edwards Street. A table has been laid for tea in the shelter of a dense laurel hedge. There is an embroidered tablecloth. The china tea set is one the family brought out from Moravia. There is a vase of arum lilies under the table, and trampled grass. The scene has been carefully set: Agnes, wearing a bonnet, holding the teapot, ready to pour; Jack standing on one side of her; Joe sitting on a folding verandah chair on the other. Joe is wearing a serge jacket, waistcoat and knickerbockers. His legs are crossed; he is balancing a cup and saucer on his knee.

What can one read in the face of this sixteen-year-old? He has tilted the straw boater back on his head. His mouth is set. His gaze seems uneasy, almost shifty. He has been toughened by hard work. He is

someone who will not take kindly to being told what to do. Someone with a short fuse. Who will buck authority.

When I look at this photo, James K Baxter's line about *his* childhood comes to mind – 'the sense of having been pounded all over with a club by invisible adversaries' – and I have to caution myself not to see things in it that are not there, although sometimes the blankness and muteness of the past beg to be redeemed in the imagination of the living. As when, fifty-five years after the event, someone remembers 'this awful mouth, vile mouth he had, cruel as though he'd fire at you as quick as look at you, you know he had that type, a bad look' ... so claiming, as we all so readily do, wisdom with hindsight.

In the winter of 1905, Joe Pawelka is working for a butcher in Dannevirke on the eastern side of the Ruahine range. He writes home to his mother:

> *My Dear Mother,*
> *I suppose you are wondering where in the world I have got here in a place a little smaller than Palmerston Since I came here I have got a job butchering in the town and intend to stick to it if I dont have a row with the boss This place is not so bad to live in and since I have been here I have met Cruden and his missus the Richardsons and the Gensons who are all living here Cruden is as big a skiter as ever he was his Mrs has grown like her mother about as broad as she is long Well Mother how have you been getting on I hope you are quite happy and well and am not working too hard I suppose the kid gives you enough bother though Oh Mother what about the Photo you promised me I should like to have a separate one of the lot of you Agnes Jack and yourself Tell Agnes to get her Photo taken as soon as she can and you too mother for I often wish for a separate Photo of you all so try and satisfy my wish if you can I hope you got that Photo of mine all right I have been wondering weather it went astray or not Dear Mother I wonder whether you have been why I asked for my school certificate in such a hurry for the truth is I had a chance of obtaining a government billet as Guard on the Railway train at Masterton, but I would not take the billet on account of the wages too small If I had been 21 years of age I would have received 8 shillings a day to*

start but being young they would not give enough to suit me and so I threw it up I have been travelling about aimlessly ever since and as you see luck brought me here and I struck work at my own trade Dear Mother you always complained about Kimbolton being a cold place but I believe this is worse here I do not know if it is always like this but the weather is something terrible since I have been here I have seen three snow falls all ready. I suppose Kimbolton is nearly as bad now too I am glad I am not in that miserable hole I wonder when I shall see it again How is young Jack getting on I expect he is getting quite a big lump of a fellow by this time and the baby too you havent told me its name yet Mother I feel quite proud to have a little sister like that Have you got a Go Cart for her yet If not write and let me know How are all the people getting on around you now I expect ~~you wou~~ if I were to go back I should find nearly all strangers in the town and all the young fellows married by what I have heard on occasions The fools are mad and dont know what they are doing never mind we have all got to go through the mill once they find women out as well as I have they wont trouble their heads about them How is Agnes getting on with the tailoring it is a good thing for her to learn something in that line it is far easier than going out to service Well Mother it is getting dark and I cant very well see to write I would like to tell you a little more but I cant see so I think I shall close this little letter I hope to hear from you as soon as possible so write immediately and let it be a long letter with any amount of news in it Good by Dear Mother my best love to you and Agnes and Jack

    from
        Your loving Son
        J Pawelka

The Blind Impress

Written five weeks before he turned eighteen, the letter is from a solitary young man with little joy in his life. It is the one window we have on his world at this age. With the exception of his family, his hometown holds no redeeming memories for him. His father does not figure in his affections. His unhappiness has embittered him, making him cynical and judgemental. He has a habit of getting into arguments with employers, and changes jobs often. And he has been wounded in love. The world is a dark, inhospitable place.

☙❧

3

The Other Side of the Tracks

Henry James once observed that for any writer 'there is the story of one's hero, and then, thanks to the intimate connection of things, the story of one's story itself.'

As I began to piece together the mosaic of Joe Pawelka's early life my thoughts went back to the small Taranaki town where I was raised. It was no more a 'miserable hole' than Joe's Kimbolton, or any small town anywhere. There are thousands of Moabites in the world, and there is no reason to slight them. They contain as many happy and unhappy families as any city. Still, they're the kinds of places you don't want to get stuck in. And if you're young, and have known no other life, you have to get away. To find yourself. To come into your own.

There was another reason why Moabite became implicated in my attempt to understand Joe Pawelka's beginnings. Moabite was built on Ngati-Maru land confiscated by the government in 1863 to punish the insurgent Taranaki tribes, defray the costs of the military campaign against Wiremu Kingi, and provide land for settlers. Through one of those tragic ironies of which history is replete, at the very moment that the Ngati-Maru lands on the Upper Waitara River and its tributaries were being alienated, ethnic Poles in Northern Germany were being subject to draconian assimilation laws. Under the Prussian administration, Polish towns, streets, and family names were to be Germanised. The Polish language was banned in the schools, land was seized, military conscription enforced. Resistance meant certain unemployment and the loss of one's civil rights. Together with others, already landless and exploited, the Poles chose to immigrate. Thus, the dispossessed in one hemisphere unwittingly became dispossessors in another.

When Moabite first appeared on the map in the 1870s its inhabitants numbered as many Polish as English families. The Poles were Catholic; the English were Protestant.

I grew up in a state house in the still largely Polish part of town. Our neighbours had names like Fabish, Dodunski, Bielski, Schimanski and Kuklinski. And jokes were told about the curious mix of Polish and Anglo names: Drinkwater, Haverbier, Schicker, Biesiek.

Of course, the joking wasn't all innocent.

'Catholic wogs, stink like dogs.'

The gibes of kids echoed the voice of age-old bigotry and intolerance, and from an early age I remember feeling that there was something amiss in the fact that the kids with Polish names were poor and attended the Catholic school, while most of my classmates were Protestant and Anglo. It was like that other division, suspected but seldom spoken of, between Pakeha and Maori. In the whitebait season, black-clad kuia came up from Waitara with flax kits bulging with whitebait. They had moko on their chins, and smoked pipes. They sat, shawls drawn around their shoulders, on benches outside the post office or on the kerbstones. At night they vanished. But you never heard talk of confiscated land; only of some so-called superstition that made Maoris afraid of Moabite because it lay on the route Mount Taranaki would take when it returned from exile and rejoined the other mountains in the middle of the island.

I hadn't been back to Moabite for many years. But in Wellington, racking my brains for anything that might help me understand Joe Pawelka, I found myself recalling my last trip home.

It would be wrong to say this trip was a pilgrimage. Yet, if the truth be told, who does not return to the neighbourhoods and landscapes of childhood without a sense of nostalgia that deepens into a sense of loss.

Most of my old friends had moved on. The house in which I grew up had fallen into disrepair. And the town's familiar landmarks – the band rotunda, the cenotaph, the railway station, the municipal library and offices – were surrounded by new buildings and looked anomalous. As for the streets, they were as empty as ever, and it was only by reminding myself how our lives unfold and fall apart behind closed doors that I could believe that this place had the highest rate of violent crime in the nation.

It was early afternoon when I went into the Railway Hotel and ordered a double vodka. The barman was nobody known to me, so I took my drink to a corner table where the sun filtered through the painted DB sign on the windowpane like the amber light of cathedral glass.

I did not expect to run into anyone I knew, and was scribbling in my journal when Eddie Potroz came up behind me and clamped a heavy hand on my shoulder.

I recognised Eddie at once. The birthmark like a blackberry stain across one side of his face. His self-abnegating manner.

Our conversation was forced. As though we were sparring. Parrying blows.

'What are you doing now?'

'Keepin' outta trouble. How about you?'

'Getting around.'
'I haven't seen you since, when was it?'
'It must have been our school reunion?'
'That was it!'

We drank vodka all afternoon, and shot some pool. We remembered how we used to play marbles together along the dirt footpath of Moa Street or at school, incising a circle in the clay, the outline of an eye, and beating the other kids hands-down. We used to swap glass mandalas and tors. And we always walked home from school together along the Manutahi stream, so we could wash and appraise our hoard in the icy water.

Eddie lived with his mother in a cottage behind a huge lawsoniana hedge. A passage ran through the house from front door to back. The floorboards sagged on rotting piles. There was torn linoleum in the kitchen, and sugar bags for door mats. But it was my second home, where I read the *Superman* and *Captain Marvel* comics my parents banned.

As we reminisced, we talked of our need for heroes. While other boys sought glory on the rugby field, our triumphs lay in larceny and subterfuge. On Prize Days, as some dignitary droned on about the virtues of team spirit and patriotism, we hatched subversive schemes to raid the tennis club for soft drinks and biscuits, or climb the huge rhododendron tree in the middle of town and eavesdrop on the old codgers who spent their days in its shade. Our friendship was forged in the shared if mistaken belief that we were misfits, and that nothing we could do would ever gain acceptance or win approval.

We were addicted to the movies. Hollywood licensed our sense of difference. We took our personae from the electric shadows, as well as our names: Tom Mix. Flash Gordon. From B-grade films we learned how to smoke, fight, drink martinis with a sophisticated sneer, and wear a raincoat even when it wasn't raining. We never got the message that crime does not pay.

Eddie quit school when he was fifteen and went to New Plymouth. Though we were of an age, the fact that I was still in short pants and school uniform and he was riding a motorbike and flashing money around ended our intimacy.

But meeting again after so many years, the gap closed. Eddie told me how he'd got into trouble, converting cars, joy-riding, 'that sort of thing. Didn't harm no one.' But he got caught and did time. He didn't like to talk about it much. It was like it had happened to someone else. Anyway, he had paid his dues. Now he was married, with two kids. That was all that mattered.

Looking back, I think our need for heroism was driven by a deeper need to give dignity to our sense of being different. We needed to mythologise our marginality. We were duffers at school. We were no good at sports. We were, or thought we were, pariahs. It was the old story of not feeling accepted, and not wanting to risk further hurt by seeking acceptance. In fact, you go out of your way to avoid the humiliation of being knocked back. So you withdraw. Or form an alliance with someone who feels as you do. For a while you gain a sense of spurious dignity in defiance, in going against the grain, in brooding on your sense of otherness. But it's a lost cause. You paint yourself into a corner, and become more and more vulnerable as you secretly dream of acceptance by beating the others at their own game.

Perhaps this is why, even now, I have recurring dreams of our school cricket field on a summer afternoon, and see myself running in to bowl, or feel my sinews strain as I crack the leather ball through the covers for a six. But, as with Eddie Potroz, there's little consolation in the memory of one's misdemeanours, and I have to go back to a winter morning when I was eight to focus on the one highpoint of all my schooldays.

Since ours was a small country school, almost everyone played together at recess. Usually Bedlam, or Running Through.

'Running Through' began with a kid standing in the middle of the playground and trying to tackle someone as the whole school rushed from one side to the other. If you were tackled and brought down, you went into the middle. So the odds quickly turned against anyone running this gauntlet and getting through. On this particular day I was one of the last who had not been tackled. Those of us who had survived now lined up and faced the rest of the school. There seemed no way through the forest of jeering faces. But I hurtled across the playground, dodging, stumbling, wincing, and found myself within a couple of yards of the other side. At the very moment I thought I would make it, Jenkins and Mumby materialised in front of me. They were giants. Thirteen-year-olds still stuck in Standard Six. Front-row forwards in the first fifteen. Bigger and more belligerent than most of our teachers, they saw me coming, crouched and joined their arms – forming a barred gate against my progress. But then, as though lifted out of myself, I leapt over their locked arms, landed beyond them, and made it home. As I turned to take in what I had accomplished so miraculously, I met with looks of surprise and approval. Then they both came up to me, so tall they blotted out the sun, and shook my hand, and said I was really something. It was my finest hour.

When I read of Joe Pawelka's ability to jump, how can I not remember this incident? And is it not also inevitable that when I try to imagine him, I think of Eddie Potroz, and what he had to say about acceptance?

'Dad did a bunk,' Eddie told me. 'I used to think he was Christmas, but he was a shit. I never want to do to my kids what he did to Mum and me.'

'Did you ever see him again?'

'Yeah, he dropped in from time to time.'

Eddie's father was what my grandmother called 'a bad seed'. Perhaps he was one of the miscreants my grandfather had to put in the lock-up from time to time, someone my grandmother grudgingly had to provide dinner and breakfast for. For all I know, it might have been my grandfather who put Eddie's father away.

There is something unforgiving about a small town. It's not simply the judgemental attitude, the oppressive moralising, the inescapable gossip that condemns anyone who deviates from the straight and narrow. It's more to do with the impossibility of hiding anything, or of forgetting. I think of Eddie's mother, for instance, as she struggled to make ends meet. Neither the object of scorn nor of sympathy, she bore her misfortunes like a stigma, as irrevocable as Eddie's birthmark. And I think of Miss Therkelson, whose lover jilted her when she was seventeen. In despair, she threw herself from the top of a drowned quarry outside the town, and smashed her hip on the submerged carcass of an old truck. She limped around Moabite for the rest of her life, her ugly injury a permanent reminder of something which would have been best forgotten. And I think of Cloris Goller, who had a child out of wedlock, and, in my grandmother's words, 'lost her hold on goodness'. She carried the burden of her 'mistake' for as long as she lived, and saw her daughter, Clover, grow up to be as beautiful as she had been, then follow in her footsteps, 'duffed', we heard it said, 'by some milkbar cowboy'. What chance did one have, when every primary school child knew the 'full story', and passed it on.

You were damned if you stayed, and you were often damned if you didn't. But at least in clearing out there was some hope of making a fresh start.

I used to think I was damned, just by being born in Moabite. But when I was fifteen, everything changed. My aunt from America came to stay.

She'd gone to California on a working holiday when she was twenty and never come home. Now, with her sons married and her husband dead, she'd decided to look up old family and see the world she'd left twenty-eight years before.

She took my breath away. Her raunchy and irrepressible laughter. Her cocktail before dinner. Her Camel cigarettes. The way she said sidewalk instead of footpath, tomeighta instead of tomato. The way she shared her anecdotes of Mexico and Greece with me. On her second day with us, she took over the kitchen and baked a moussaka. Looking back, I wonder if she wasn't, in some sly way, taking her revenge on the town that had given her such a rough time when she was in her teens. I like to think that she was proving something to herself, something that had weighed on her mind for twenty-eight years: that you could take the provisions available in our local grocer's shop and subversively turn them into something exotic. Something out of this world.

I remember going downtown with her to buy the meat for the moussaka.

She asked Mr Muldoon for a pound of ground lamb.

'What's ground lamb?'

'Minced lamb.'

'You don't mince lamb.'

'What do you mean you don't mince lamb? Haven't you got a mincer?'

'I've never heard of mincing lamb.'

'Then just give me the lamb. I'll mince it myself.'

'What would you want to mince lamb for?'

'A moussaka.'

'A moose what?'

At dinner we picked at the exotic mush our aunt spooned onto our plates. My older sister said it smelled funny. My father said he did not like the eggplant. My younger sisters said yuck, and pushed their plates away. But I tucked in, and asked for seconds, and added to my mother's humiliation by declaring that it was the best meal I had ever eaten in my life.

Was this the sort of thing that made my destiny different from Eddie Potroz's? Or was it that I preferred to read the Classics rather than Classic Comics? Or are all such comparisons equally unrevealing?

Joe Pawelka never escaped. Not in the way I did. Not even in the way Eddie did.

Joe's one surviving letter ends with the winter light failing. 'I would like to tell you a little more,' he writes to his mother, 'but I can't see.'

When we are young and confused, can we ever expect to see clearly? And when we are older, and think we possess the clarity of hindsight, can we honestly say we remember the way things were?

I tell myself that it probably isn't a matter of seeing clearly at all, but of using the imagination to repair and augment our vision – which is always faulty. And what I imagine, when I think of Joe Pawelka and the town where I was raised, is a place where identities overlap and blur, a place where one is haunted by the thought that someone else's fate might equally have been one's own, where one man's loss is another's gain, or, like the icy pool where Eddie Potroz and I washed our mandalas, a place where colours run together, and differences are eclipsed by what is shared.

CB EO

4

Of the Woe
that is in Marriage

On his twenty-first birthday, 1 August 1908, Joe Pawelka was admitted to Palmerston Public Hospital with typhoid fever. Designated a 'disease of complications', typhoid typically might cause intestinal ulcers, haemorrhaging, perforation of the bowel, peritonitis and osteomyelitis. 'Localisation and abscess formation could occur in any organ.' In Joe Pawelka's case, it was found necessary to remove an abscess from one of his lungs. In order for the patient to be able to cough and so avoid drowning in his own fluid, he needed to be conscious during surgery. So Pawelka's three operations were done with local anaesthetic. Three of his ribs and a portion of a lung were removed. His chances of surviving this trauma were fifty-fifty.

After five months in hospital, he went home to Kimbolton where his mother nursed him back to health. Two years later, during the Pawelka manhunt, our *New Zealand Times* reporter would be told that Joe had been 'a marvellous patient' – a remark which justified the conclusion that the determination and fortitude that brought Joe through his illness would now help him survive life in the open. Others expressed the opinion that Joe's mind had been 'deranged' by the ordeal he had undergone in hospital.

After convalescing in Kimbolton for a couple of months, Joe began work at Banks & Co., a butchery on The Square in Palmerston. Four months later, on 3 July 1909, the shop manager, Leonard Hampton, sacked him because he 'found him such a liar'.

Ten days after being thrown out of work, Joe allegedly broke into Arthur Dixon's butcher's shop and stole 120 lbs of bacon and a steel. Three weeks later he burgled the house of a Palmerston lawyer, Harold Cooper, taking a pair of silver hairbrushes, a dinner suit, a shaving case and a cigar case.

The following month, on 29 September, he married Hannah Elizabeth Wilson at Ashhurst. Lizzie was twenty-eight, Joe twenty-two.

Hannah Elizabeth Wilson (Lizzie) sometime before her marriage to Joe Pawelka.

Assuming they had not known each other before Joe's illness, they probably met in Palmerston, sometime between March and August 1909. It was a brief courtship. Joe was in and out of work. And already, it seems, he was in trouble.

The couple rented a house in Palmerston at Church Street west, and Joe took up his old job at the abattoirs. Sometime during the first month of the marriage, Lizzie got pregnant. But – according to newspaper reports six months later – the Pawelkas' 'married life was unhappy', and their 'domestic affairs appear to have been very unpleasant'. In early December, Lizzie filed a court application for 'summary separation', and returned to live with her widowed mother in Ashhurst.

Lizzie sometime after the breakup of her marriage and the birth of her daughter Iris.

Joe's response was a rather pathetic attempt at suicide in a shallow pool in the Manawatu River. Brought before a local magistrate on 13 December, his counsel – ironically, the lawyer whose house he'd broken into four and a half months earlier – argued that Joe's severe illness had affected his general health. As if in compliance with this argument, in court Joe acted 'in a very peculiar manner'. After admitting his guilt, separation from Lizzie was ordered. Discharged without a conviction, he had to pay court costs as well as wife support of ten shillings a week, the first payment due 10 January.

About a week after his court appearance, Joe moved into a boarding-house in Cuba Street.

Why did Lizzie walk out on Joe? What turned her against him?

Certainly they can't have known each other very well when they married. And it seems likely that Joe was guilty of petty larceny during the period when they were living in Church Street.* Perhaps Lizzie was suddenly confronted with the sinister side of her husband. His possession of a revolver, which he seemed to regard as an extension of himself, may have hastened her decision to leave him. There is the possibility that he made violent threats, if not against her then against himself. Perhaps he was jealous of the hold her mother had over her. Perhaps he wanted to possess her utterly, like a bird in a cage.

His attempted suicide got him no sympathy. Instead, it saddled him with maintenance and court costs which he was probably hard-pressed to pay. But if Lizzie's decision was irrevocable, so too was his resolution. The callow eighteen-year-old who had written that marriage was for fools who didn't know what they were doing, and women not worth the trouble they brought, now found himself bereft. Unable to imagine or endure life without Lizzie, he began to fill the Church Street house with stolen furniture and furnishings, as if seeking to make good his emotional loss through material gain.

Such a metaphorical fusion of feelings and things is familiar to most of us. After a death or divorce, people often squabble over the spoils as though, in laying claim to things, they will magically recover their sundered lives. Or, when a house is burgled, people feel sullied and bereft, as if their very bodies and souls had been invaded. Through what we *possess* we fetishistically establish our sense of who we *are*.

---

* Joe would be charged with stealing a lady's bicycle on 9 October from Ira Gordon, a painter and paperhanger who lived a few doors away.

This may shed some light on why Joe Pawelka filled the house in Church Street with stolen furniture. The empty house embodied his loss. It also served as a sore reminder of the bourgeois world in which he had failed to find a place. If he filled his house with things taken from the family homes of others, perhaps, he imagined, his stolen happiness would be restored. Though *he* had failed to win Lizzie, perhaps the accoutrements of gentility would do the trick. When Hampton sacked him, he began stealing. Now that his wife has rejected him, and he has lost everything, he will stop at nothing to get her back. What does he have to lose?

Interior of typical middle-class home, Manawatu 1904.

Early on the morning of 25 February 1910, there was a 'disturbance' in the house at 107 Church Street west. Apparently Lizzie had returned to the house with her mother to collect some of her belongings. Joe was also there, and they argued.

A constable was called to the house at 8 a.m. but saw nothing to justify action. Later in the morning, however, between 11 and noon, Lizzie went to the police station and laid a complaint against her husband. Joe followed her. At the police station, in Joe's presence, she claimed he had a revolver in his possession. Husband and wife were interviewed in separate rooms. Lizzie said she wanted police protection while she removed her belongings from the house. The police denied her request, but promised to detain Joe while she went about her business.

Questioned by the police, Joe admitted having a revolver, and offered to hand it in. As soon as Lizzie and her mother left the house, Constable King went there with Joe. After the pretence of a search, Joe said he could not find his revolver, so later that afternoon, between 5 and 6, Constables King and Barry returned to the house to search for it themselves. During their search they recognised paintings stolen over the Christmas holidays from several local homes. They placed Joe Pawelka under arrest and called in detectives to investigate further.

Early next morning, accompanied by Joe and some of the citizens who had been burgled, the police resumed their search of the house. It quickly became clear that almost everything in the house was stolen property, including Joe's revolver. Ira Gordon's bicycle was in the washhouse. The steel from Dixon's butchery was found in a kitchen drawer. Harold Cooper's dinner suit, dressing case, collar-box portmanteau and set of razors came to light. Edward Kidd helped detectives identify furniture stolen from his house between Christmas Eve and 26 January – the period he and his family had been away on holiday. A Palmerston carpenter, Norman Metcalfe, who'd spent Christmas at Foxton with his family, identified items from his house. Then there was a clock belonging to James Robbie, who'd also been out of town during the Christmas break; tyres and cigars from J.B. Clarkson's warehouse; and numerous articles taken on Boxing Day from Mrs Hardley's residence: an oak table, a chair, cushions, pictures, table cover, brush stand and mirror, glass stand, vases, watch cases, carpet squares, hearth rugs, mats, fender, bedstead, silver, crockery, pots and kettles. Finally, goods stolen from Helen McKay, an unmarried dressmaker, were found: curtains, sheets, pillows and pillow cases, table cover, quilt, cushions, possum skin rug, hammock and sheepskin mats. The discovery of these items was particularly incriminating. Helen McKay's house at 1 Campbell Street was immediately behind the boarding-house in Cuba Street where Joe Pawelka was living on 3 January 1910. That night, between midnight and 1 a.m., the McKay house had been wilfully burned to the ground.

At 8 a.m. on 26 February 1910, Joe Pawelka was charged on five counts of breaking, entering and theft from the homes of Kidd, Metcalfe, Robbie, and Hardley, and from J.B. Clarkson's warehouse. When the first charge was read, Joe was heard to declare, 'Oh, good God.' When the second was read, his response was 'Good God Almighty'. To the remaining three charges he made no reply.

He was remanded in custody until 7 March, when he was further charged with breaking, entering and theft from Cooper's residence and Dixon's butchery. Finally, on 14 March, he was charged with breaking and entering the McKay house, as well as arson. He was committed for trial at the next sitting of the Palmerston North Supreme Court on 23 March.

It is now part of the Pawelka legend that Joe's troubles stemmed from his marriage. Filling his house with stolen furniture and furnishings was, it is supposed, a desperate stratagem to please and impress Lizzie, whose mother thought her daughter had married beneath her. Though the Wilsons were also working-class migrants, in Mrs Wilson's eyes her son-in-law was a mere butcher, without manners or prospects. If Joe was to win Lizzie's heart, so this argument goes, he would have to break the hold her mother had over her. Failing that, he would have to become worthy of her by giving her the material things that defined, for her and her mother, conspicuous membership of the middle-class. Without the means to do this honestly, he resorted to theft. Or, at the very least, received or paid money for stolen property.

This comes close to Joe's own story: he claimed he'd purchased the furniture from Archie McRae, unaware it was stolen, and this had been the start of all his troubles.

The stories are plausible. There seems no doubt that Joe was besotted by Lizzie and heartbroken when she spurned him. If he was desperate enough to try to drown himself as a way of winning her back, he would have been distracted enough not to think too deeply about his dealings with Archie McRae.

And Lizzie was pregnant with their child.

But his problems predate his marriage, and it is unlikely that Archie McRae was responsible for all the criminal acts with which Joe Pawelka was charged. The theft of Ira Gordon's bicycle and Arthur Dixon's steel, the 350 cigars stolen from Clarkson's warehouse, and the theft of such gentlemanly appurtenances as a cigar case, a shaving case and dinner suit from Harold Cooper all seem to have been his doing. As for the fire which destroyed Helen McKay's house, the evidence is circumstantial but compelling: furnishings stolen from McKay's on the night of the fire were found in Pawelka's Church Street house.

Perhaps like this fire, which smouldered for some time before bursting into flame, Joe Pawelka nursed resentments and grievances that he could no longer contain. Yet it is seldom possible to half identify, let alone trace home, the blind impress all our behavings bear, and, often, all one can confidently demonstrate are the unforeseen consequences of an ill-considered act. Or draw comparisons between one's own life and that of another, endeavouring to find the common ground where an essay in human understanding might begin.

☙❧

5

Manawatu

I remember it as a place of wind and rain. A landscape laid open to the sky. Sodden paddocks, bitten by huddled herds. In winter the stench of silage. Sheep dotted over dark green hills. I used to feel that the land had been emptied of life. Walking along a valley road, your footsteps echoed in the emptiness. Except for a creek spilling down a hillside, the whistling of birds, and the *maaa maaa* of a sheep, there was a cold silence.

For the Rangitāne people, the word *manawa-tū* conjures up the legendary figure of Hau-nui-a-Nanaia. Hau's stamping ground was the west coast, but when his wife, Wairaka, ran away with another man, Hau set off in pursuit. He travelled from Whanganui (large river mouth), to Turakina (thrown down) where he bridged the river with a dead tree. Footsore, he then came to the Rangitīkei (day of trudging) where he rested overnight. Next day he journeyed south and came to the Manawatu River, flowing through a deep cleft (te Apiti) in the range and on across the flatlands to the sea. As he stepped into the cold water, Hau's breath was knocked out of him. Whence: Manawatū (breath stopped).

When I lived in the Manawatu I liked to think it was not only the coldness of the river which made Hau's heart miss a beat, but the light flooding through the gorge on a winter's day, as from a gate in the sky.

For the less mythologically-minded, the region may be conceived as a parallelogram, with the Tararua-Ruahine ranges defining its eastern side, and the sore-footed Rangitikei River to the west. Draining this uplifted land are the Oroua and Pohangina Rivers whose parallel valleys open onto the plains of the Manawatu to the south.

For Joe Pawelka there were two cardinal points: Kimbolton, which overlooks the southern plain, and Ashhurst, under the axial range, hard by the entrance to the gorge. For six weeks now, these places will determine his bearings and define his limits.

The police cells where Pawelka is detained are notoriously cramped, unventilated and unsanitary. Locally they are known as the Black Hole of Calcutta.

Ten minutes after noon on Saturday, 12 March 1910, Pawelka breaks out of the 'black hole'. Momentarily unguarded while being transferred to a more secure wing, he seizes his opportunity. Placing two buckets against the galvanised iron fence which encloses the exercise yard, he clambers up onto the roof, then jumps down into the United Farmers' yard next door. There he takes an employee's bicycle and disappears into Boundary Road.

The police immediately alert Ashhurst and warn Lizzie. It is thought that he will 'resort to extreme violence upon her, by reason of her connection with the circumstances which led to his arrest.' But he heads north, along the main highway.

Eight hours after his escape, he is spotted near the Awahuri abattoirs, leading the police to suspect that he has taken shelter in the house of a Mrs Wicks, 'with whom he had been intimate before his marriage'. By midnight he is in Bunnythorpe where he enters Rowe's store with a soft brown felt hat pulled down over his eyes, and buys biscuits and lemonade. He pays with a pound note and asks if he can borrow some carbide for his bicycle lamp which, Rowe observes, is tied to the handlebars with binder twine.

By dawn on Sunday he has reached the Kiwitea stream, just east of Feilding. He catches some sleep on a shingle bank shaded by willows, where the river loops back by the bridge. At 11 a.m. he walks along the stream bed to a contractor's camp where he cadges a meal. He then returns to his hiding place.

That night he continues north on his stolen bicycle, stealing two loaves of bread, four pounds of uncooked beef, and some jam and syrup from a road contractor near Kimbolton. The police stake out the Pawelka house in Edwards Street. At 3.30 in the morning the fugitive tries to slip past them, but is seen. Clambering onto his bicycle, he speeds away down the long hill from Kimbolton. The police, unable to stop him, fire shots into the air as he is swallowed up by the darkness.

Six hours later, a police sergeant finds telltale cycle tyre tracks in the shingle by the Kiwitea bridge. Then he sees Pawelka 150 yards ahead. Joe flees down the road toward Feilding. He goes along Derby Street into East Street, thence to Aorangi, avoiding the town centre. At Aorangi he turns down Cameron's Line in the direction of Awahuri. A quarter of a mile from the Awahuri abattoir, he abandons his bicycle by the roadside and strikes out across country. At 2.20 that afternoon, two constables standing under the verandah at the Awahuri store see him walk past. He has a handkerchief pulled up over his face, but is readily identified. When arrested and handcuffed he offers no resistance, and says he will go quietly.

An hour and a half after his capture, he is brought before S.M. Thompson in the Magistrate's Court in Palmerston. Thompson orders him remanded in custody in the Terrace Gaol, Wellington, until 23 March.

At the time of his escape, Joe Pawelka was confused. At first he may have reckoned on help in Awahuri, possibly from workmates at the abattoirs. But then he travelled east, to Bunnythorpe, as if he had taken it into his head to go to Ashhurst and see Lizzie. At this point, however, he turned north for home. Thwarted by a police ambush in Kimbolton, he headed south again, winding up at Awahuri where he began.

It seems he has nowhere to hide. Worse, there is no one to whom he can turn. Perhaps he does not resist recapture because he has exhausted every possibility of remaining free. Indeed, one wonders whether anyone, apart from his family, is prepared to help him now. One feels that he is already beyond the pale, inspiring suspicion and fear more often than compassion. A telling detail in a newspaper account of his arrest is that he was wearing an overcoat stolen from a man called Anderson who worked at the abattoirs. Is he now feeling despised and rejected by friends, just as he felt abandoned by Lizzie? And is theft once more his way of avenging himself against those who turn their backs on him in his hour of need?

For a person badly hurt by life, even indifference may be experienced as a slight. More tragically, it may be taken as a sign of a conspiracy against one's right to justice and happiness.

CB ED

6

Fires of No Return

The sky was like lead. The southerly beat about the city like the sea. Walking along the bay, I saw yachts torn like gulls from the hold of the harbour. The wind-sheered water was all scud and wake.

It was my fourth day in Wellington. At the National Archives, gale-force winds pummelled the building; rain was flung against the windows like scattershot. Driven inward, I worked in silence on criminal record books, depositions, and police files.

In 1910, Palmerston is a town of 12,000. Under cloudy skies, a New Zealand blue ensign snaps in the wind. The business premises along Rangitikei Street are built solidly of wood or brick. Wooden telegraph poles, cross bars studded with porcelain insulators, line an unpaved street. Some men in three-piece suits and hats stand on a street corner. Several women in straw boaters and long skirts cross the road. There is no evidence of motor vehicles; only drays and carts pulled by teams of horses, and cyclists wearing cloth caps. The crimes and misdemeanours one reads about in the police court column of *The Manawatu Evening Standard* seem quaint: drunks using indecent language, bicycles without lights, truancy, vagrancy, petty

The Blind Impress

theft, rigged scales and false weights, negligence in paying maintenance, cruelty to horses, failure to keep livestock under control.

Kimbolton is like a scaled-down version of Palmerston. The main street is rutted and stony. Wooden storefronts are emblazoned with the proprietors' names: R.U. Harden's Land Stock Financial & Commission Agent; Barlow Brothers' Plumbers & Tinsmiths; the Kimbolton Saddlery; C.J. Hansen's General Store; Lowes' Family and Commercial Hotel.

In the cleared valleys of the Oroua and Pohangina Rivers, scrub is reclaiming the ransacked hillsides. There are cottages, sheds and haybarns along narrow gravel roads. Fences and grassed paddocks. A horse-drawn cart, loaded with a stack of milled boards, stands outside a farrier's. A dray carrying milk churns lurches down a metal road toward the cooperative butter factory.

It is Wednesday 23 March 1910. In Wellington, Joe Pawelka has been in custody for nine days.

At 9.30 in the morning he is in a cell in the lock-up at Lambton Quay police station with another remand prisoner, waiting to be brought before the Magistrate. The second prisoner is being held on charges of wife-desertion.

The watchhouse-keeper is twenty-six-year-old Constable J.J. Gallagher, promoted to the position only four months ago. Gallagher gives the cell key to Constable Mahoney, who takes the second prisoner to the watchhouse. But the lock on the cell door is faulty, and to compound the problem Mahoney fails to shoot the bolt home. Joe Pawelka slips out of the cell, scales a wall and is free.

In the following days, newspapers report Pawelka heading northeast into the Wairarapa where the police search is least intense, then making his way back to the Manawatu. But these reports are based on a single sighting, two days after Pawelka's escape, by a settler at Waingawa, three or four miles out of Masterton. The settler said that a man answering Pawelka's description called at his house and asked for food. After finishing his meal, the stranger rode away on a bicycle.

It is likely that this visitor was one of the thousands of vagrants or itinerant workers who drifted around the country in these years. If this was a case of mistaken identity, it would not be the last. In the weeks ahead, every nondescript stranger or derelict will be Pawelka, and the identity of the fugitive assimilated to that of the swagger who, since the depression of the 1880s and early 1890s, had become a familiar figure in the social landscape. One must remember that these were insular and isolated communities where footloose young men and vagrants were often the object of scorn and the focus of parochial fears.

According to Pawelka's own account, he knew the police would concentrate their search on the Wellington railway station and wharves, so he decided against making for the railway yards. Instead, he walked to Wadestown, forded a stream to Crofton, stole a bicycle and rode north via Johnsonville. That night he slept in an old shed at Titahi Bay. Next day he went on to Paekakariki, and late in the afternoon climbed into an empty cattle truck on a goods train going north. He got off at Longburn, four miles southwest of Palmerston, and hid there for a couple of days, surviving on bread, cheese and tinned sardines he stole from Charles Perry's store on Saturday night. He also helped himself to cigarettes and a change of clothing. Then he made his way along the Manawatu River and up Stoney Creek to a prepared hiding place in the creek bed of McRae's farm.

How was he described?

According to Constable Gallagher the escaped prisoner had dark hair, black eyes, was clean-shaven, sallow, of slim build, and walked erect with a quick stride. Gallagher also recalled that Pawelka was dressed in light green trousers, a soft white shirt, blucher boots, a dark coat, but no hat or collar. A 'wanted' poster, circulated the day after the escape, included a photo of the fugitive taken against a weatherboard wall.

Powelka is colonial born, twenty-eight years of age, standing 5 ft 10 inches in height, and weighs about 10 st 10 lb. He is of pale, sallow complexion, with a thin face, sunken cheeks, dark brown hair, dark eyebrows, and is usually clean-shaven. At the time of his escape he had about ten days' growth of hair on his face. He was dressed in brown tweed trousers, and a soft shirt. He had no vest or cap, though since his escape he may have acquired these articles or changed his wearing apparel.

His age is given incorrectly. But something else is amiss. The complexity of Joe Pawelka's life has been reduced to a mug-shot, a negative caricature. The frozen pose with its formal placement of the hands, the prisoner literally up against a wall, evokes an image of a body in death. Made over as a criminal type, he suffers our gaze and our judgement. His identity, his history, his background, his thoughts, his voice have been invalidated. Whatever unsettled and troubled his soul, the axis of his misfortunes now shifts to the world around him. Trapped inside the photo as in a cage, his only freedom now will be to become the person he has been made.

There is never any respite. On the run you are nerve-racked by lack of sleep and the unrelenting need for vigilance. There is no safe house, no haven. You can't simply lie low or sit still. It is like being lost. You are driven from cover, not only by fear of your pursuers closing in, but by the pain and disquiet in your own mind. You move to keep at bay the inner voices of your despair.

Joe Pawelka was living rough in an autumn that was already turning to winter. Preoccupied with finding food and clothing and the exhausting search for shelter and succour, he was also a man possessed by grief. He moved continually, not only to evade capture, but to shift the burden of his loss. Alone and desperate, he seems to vacillate between imagining some kind of reconciliation with Lizzie and being overwhelmed by abject misery. Self-lacerating grief gives way to rage. He sees himself as unjustly used, an outcast, a voice crying in the wilderness. The society which has made him a pariah will now suffer for its sins. He has a score to settle. He will visit upon those who rejected him the hurt they visited upon him.

At 10.45 on the night of Saturday 2 April, nine days after Pawelka's escape, Jack and Pauline Kendall return to their house near Awapuni, west of Palmerston, after five hours shopping in town. Under a willow near the front gate they find a sugar bag of food stolen from the house. A duck, 10 lbs of bacon, 4 lbs of cake, and a small loaf of bread are wrapped in one of Pauline Kendall's tablecloths. Nearby is a small leather bag containing a jar of pickles. Inside the house they find drawers ransacked and an empty larder. Jack Kendall's first suspicion is that two boys recently escaped from the Weraroa Training Farm are responsible.

As he goes back to the gate to retrieve a candle he left there, Kendall sees a man walking down the road toward the house. Later, he will tell the police that when the man saw him he dropped into a crouch with a revolver in each hand and said: 'Your money, you —! It's your money I want!' The man was wearing a cap and old overcoat. Over his eyes and the upper part of his face he wore a mask made from one of Pauline Kendall's black silk blouses. His mouth was covered with a neckerchief. When Kendall explained that he'd spent all his pay in town, the armed man (who he now suspected to be Pawelka because of 'a hissing tone which is a peculiarity of Powelka's utterance') allegedly declared, 'You don't think they're loaded, eh?' and threatened to blow Kendall's brains out, brandishing the pistols in front of his eyes and rubbing his cheeks with the cold steel. Terrified, Kendall turned out his pockets.

When Pauline Kendall came out to see what was going on, Pawelka ordered her back to the house to fetch her purse. When he found it empty, the intruder lost his temper. 'You think these are not loaded, do you?' he said, and promptly fired one of the revolvers within a foot of Pauline Kendall's head. She fell back against the fence, screaming, and went on screaming for two or three minutes until a cyclist suddenly appeared out of the darkness of the road. Immediately the intruder fell into a crouch, crept along the fenceline, dropped into a ditch and disappeared.

Though Kendall knew Pawelka well (they'd both worked at the abattoirs and often broke their cheques together on Saturday nights), there was considerable doubt whether Kendall's identification of Pawelka's voice would be accepted by a court. Doubts were also cast on Kendall's story of being fired at.

But what bothered me, reading accounts of the hold-up, was why Pawelka's mates seemed so afraid of him, so ready to incriminate him. In a sworn statement to the Supreme Court, Jack Kendall would declare, 'I knew who he was as soon as I saw him ... it was a very clear night ... it was not dark ... I have no doubt as to the identity of the man. I could have told him a mile off.' Though Pauline Kendall, in her testimony, said she had known Pawelka 'by sight three or four months', she also 'had an idea it was Joe Powelka because of his figure. He sort of crouched down all the time.' Yet it is unlikely that Jack Kendall could have so readily recognised the man who approached his gate in darkness with his face covered. By his own admission Kendall could not clearly remember whether the intruder's overcoat and cap were grey or green. And despite having first concluded that boys from the Weraroa Training Camp had raided his wife's larder, he later told the police that his first thought had been 'Here comes Joe Powelka for a feed!' If this *was* true, why not give the fugitive a feed? If he was a workmate, why not talk to him, if only to press upon him the need to give himself up. Why not at least listen to his story?

If Joe Pawelka's own testimony is to be believed, he was never at Awapuni on the night in question, but shooting rabbits near his camp at McCrae's farm on Stoney Creek. He avowed that Awapuni was not on his beat: if he travelled between Longburn and Bunnythorpe, he skirted Palmerston to the north using the Boundary and Kairanga Roads.

In Wellington I began reading Mikal Gilmore's *A Shot in the Heart*, and was at once struck by parallels with Joe Pawelka's story.

Much of Mikal Gilmore's book concerns his brother Gary, who

gained international notoriety in 1976 and 1977 by challenging and ordering the State of Utah not to stay his execution after he had been found guilty of murder and sentenced to die. In his memoir, Mikal Gilmore searches for 'a decisive turning point', a moment in Gary's story 'where everything went wrong', 'an instance that gave birth to my family's devastation.' He asks whether this moment might be located 'inside Gary's life' or 'outside him ... in the secret darkness of his own father's history.' In the end he has to conclude that there are no simple answers, only interminable arguments and useless speculations. But then Mikal Gilmore turns to a different sort of question. No longer seeking to identify 'each terrible link in that fateful chain', he asks instead 'where could we have altered this history', how could the fateful chain have been broken and other links forged? In effect, his question turns our attention from what we cannot change to what we can.

In his last interview on Utah's death row, Gary Gilmore mentioned the name of a teacher called Tom Lyden who taught him in Portland, Oregon when he was in eighth grade. Joseph Lane Grade School had been a tough school, and when Gary Gilmore started there he already had a delinquent history as a rebel, thief and troublemaker.

The day Gary Gilmore was executed by firing squad and made his blood atonement, Tom Lyden, who'd been following the story on the news, got a call from the man who'd conducted this last interview. Lyden was surprised to hear that Gary had remembered him. He was even more surprised to learn that the condemned man had mentioned Lyden not only as the teacher he had most valued and respected, but as one of the few people he had reached out to for help. But rather than rue the extra step he might have taken twenty-five years ago with Gary Gilmore, Lyden, now principal at another school in Portland, thinks of a boy in his school who is giving his teachers trouble, and at a staff meeting the following day,

Lyden tells the boy's teachers about the phone call he'd received. 'Gary told somebody that he once had an eighth-grade teacher whom he'd held his hand out to, and that teacher didn't quite reach for it. He said he thought that perhaps that teacher could have made a difference in his life. That teacher was me. Now, what are you going to do about this youngster?'

It is Tuesday 5 April, three days after the Kendall hold-up. On this night, there are three major fires in Palmerston, and Pawelka will be blamed for them all.

The fire bell is first rung at 8 p.m. At the Boys' High School in Featherston Street, a lavatory window is smashed and a fire lit which spreads quickly through the wooden building. As the brigade is fighting this blaze, another breaks out in the newly-renovated storage, packing, polishing and upholstery rooms of W. Pegden on The Square. The brigade rushes to Pegden's, only to be summoned at 10.30 to yet another fire at the temporary premises of Millar and Giorgi's draper's shop, fifty yards away. With a horse-drawn fire-engine and an inadequate supply of water under pressure, the volunteer brigade can do little more than contain the fires.

Almost immediately rumours circulate that the fires are the work of an arsonist, and it is quickly agreed that Pawelka is 'the person responsible for the conflagrations'. Various citizens claim to have seen him in various parts of town, and by midnight Palmerston is, in the words of one newspaper man, 'practically reduced to a state of terror'. In this uneasy atmosphere, women leave their homes on the outskirts of town to stay with friends and men arm themselves with revolvers. At the same time, police reinforcements are brought in from Wanganui and Hawera.

Yet even in this panic there are voices urging caution and calm. Observes a reporter for *The New Zealand Times*, 'persons with a good knowledge of Powelka declare that he is not half as eccentric as has been made out, and that in some respects he is a man of more than ordinary intelligence. Men who have worked with him are of the opinion that his object in returning to the district is to avenge himself on his wife for having acted in such a way as to cause his arrest in the first instance.'

In the early hours of the morning after the fires, Pawelka dumps the Dayton bicycle he'd stolen from the driveway of a house near the High School and steals a horse and saddle. After crossing the Fitzherbert bridge, he makes for the Pahiatua Track. Late in the afternoon, in failing light, he rides up to a store a couple of hundred yards from the Pahiatua railway station and asks for some fuses. The store has none, and Pawelka rides away.

Two mounted constables from Palmerston then spot him on the Ballance Road and go in pursuit. Pawelka's horse has been ridden hard and is lame from having lost two shoes. With Constables King and Macleod closing on him, Pawelka abandons his horse and plunges into Matthews Bush along the Mangahao River. King glimpses the fugitive running among stumps and logs with a revolver in his hand. Pawelka is wearing a green slouch hat, a dark green tweed overcoat, and yellow leggings stolen from Millar and Giorgi's on the night of the fire. King fires at the fleeing man, but he is quickly gone.

Seeing no point in following Pawelka into the bush, King rides off to get reinforcements.

A search, beginning at first light the next day, yields nothing. It is assumed Pawelka broke through the police cordon in the night and will be making for Dannevirke where he once worked in Brighouse's butchery. Most likely, however, he emerged from the bush onto the Ballance Valley Road and made his way to Woodville where he laid low until late on the night of 8 April.

The Pahiatua district now experiences the same panic that seized Palmerston. Armed settlers volunteer to help the police search. Rumours spread like wildfire.

'The theory is gaining ground,' observes a reporter for *The New Zealand Times*, 'that some person other than Powelka is assisting to increase the present condition of unrest, as it is considered impossible for one individual to have done what is alleged to have taken place in the city and neighbourhood.'

At the end of the day I wrote down in my journal some of the things which seemed now to be falling into place.

When Joe escapes, 'wanted' notices go up on police bulletin boards around the country. The gaunt face is both bewildered and belligerent. What chances he had to define his own identity, to tell his own story, have been lost. He is already the bogeyman parents will use to frighten their errant children into line. He is doomed to travel a road which has been decided for him. But he will embrace this destiny with a vengeance. If he cannot prove his innocence, he will perversely embrace his guilt. If he cannot love, he will attract hate. He will fulfill everyone's worst expectations. Condemned by others, he will now condemn himself.

Not once during the fortnight after his escape does he turn for home. He sees himself as a man alone against the world. The change is presaged in his suicidal gestures. When crossed in his desire to be accepted, he imagines his own annihilation. There is no mystery in this. If one's need for recognition is not met through affection, it will often be sought through disaffection. We all know children who, unable to get love from their parents, turn to eliciting hate. If Joe Pawelka cannot gain recognition through conforming to social convention, he will gain it through defiance. In so far as the law diminishes him, he will become a law unto himself. He will turn the tables on the world that has turned against him. So he burns down a high school, destroying a symbol of the decent education to which he once aspired. Then burns down a furniture warehouse and draper's shop, symbolically destroying the trappings of the social class which has spurned him.

☙❧

7

Fugue

Returning from exile is a bit like returning from the dead. You half expect to re-enter the same world you left, but the connective tissue has gone; both you and the place with which you identify have changed. Strange as it may seem, this sense of loss can be more devastating than any homesickness you experience when away.

When I came back to Wellington, the city felt both alien and familiar. The concrete ziggurats and glass towers that stood shoulder to shoulder in the narrow downtown streets did not entirely eclipse my memories of what had once stood there. But I was aware that a new generation now occupied the space I had once considered mine. This had the effect of making me feel I was invisible. I moved about like a revenant.

This sense of being displaced in a place I still thought of as home influenced the way I saw Joe Pawelka. At times, it was as though the line between myself and Joe became blurred, and with this blurring went an erasure of the line between present and past.

One evening at Les and Mary Cleveland's house in Brooklyn where I was staying, Les dug out a reel of film he'd shot twenty-nine years ago. He'd never developed it. He had taken the photos in the summer of '65 when he and Mary came to stay with me and my first wife, Pauline, in the southern Wairarapa. Vince O'Sullivan and his wife, Tui, were also with us. Three couples very much in love.

Now, after all this time, Les had decided to develop the film.

The photos he brought out of his dark-room were grainy, grey and scratched. This only increased their power. It was like opening up a grave and finding no evidence of decay. The shock of seeing these snapshots overwhelmed me. They were windows onto a time I had reworked in memory. But now a faithful likeness of Pauline, who died in 1983, had reappeared, and it was like a door opened for a moment onto a field of light and then slammed shut.

Here we are, sitting outside the Lake Ferry hotel in the sun, except for Mary, who must have taken the photo. In another photo we are in the bar holding glasses of beer and peering at Mary behind the camera. Other photos capture us sitting together in long grass, somewhere near the Pinnacles, eating lunch. Here is this beautiful young woman laughing at the camera, and a callow young man, myself, beside her, draining a bottle of DB Brown, oblivious.

I remembered Michaelmas daisies shimmering in the lilac Wairarapa light. Of long evenings, walking country roads. The smell of pine needles and river water. For twenty-nine years I had remembered these things ... but the faces had become a blur.

Would there be anything like this, a photograph, a letter, that would give me a glimpse into Joe Pawelka's life?

Since Joe's escape, Lizzie and her mother have, on police advice, stayed every night in the Ashhurst hotel. It is still widely believed that Pawelka is bent on vengeance, and has 'declared his intention of shooting his wife and mother-in-law and various other people at Ashhurst.'

At 9.30 in the morning of Saturday 9 April 1910, Lizzie and Hannah return home.

Hannah Wilson's house is 'in a lonely part of Ashhurst' – the spur of a river terrace that overlooks the Pohangina Valley and the Ruahine range beyond.

Most mornings, when they get back to the house, Lizzie and her mother check to see that everything is as they left it. It is also their custom to look under the beds.

This morning, however, they remove their hats and go straight into the yard to fix the well-rope.

Lizzie hears a noise in the house. She thinks it might be the cat, but wants to make sure. She asks her mother to go and investigate. Hannah Wilson walks into the kitchen and finds herself face to face with her son-in-law.

Joe is standing with his back to the fireplace. 'Don't be afraid, Mother,' he says.

He doesn't get a chance to say anything more. In a panic, Hannah Wilson runs screaming toward her neighbour's house. Joe bolts, clambers over a fence, and seeks the shelter of the river flats below the house.

When the police arrive five minutes later and search the place, they find Pawelka's heavy fur-lined coat hanging on the back fence. It was an expensive coat. Joe bought it when he was living with Lizzie. She'd argued that they couldn't afford it, but he'd bought it anyway. To impress her? To transcend his background?

In the pockets of the coat are some .22 cartridges and detonator caps, as well as the piece of wire with which Joe had picked the back door lock.

Inside the house, it is found that Hannah Wilson's bed has been slept in. But against the assumption that Pawelka occupied it, Constable Watts argues that when he inspected the house just before daybreak there was no sign of life.

What is Joe Pawelka thinking of? What draws him back to the one place that is going to be most closely watched? What dire necessity overcomes all sense of caution, and makes him take this risk?

One clue is a note he scrawls with the lead of a bullet and leaves in a milk billy on the gatepost of the Grammars' house on the outskirts of Ashhurst. A boy called Robert Elliott, who lives with the Grammars, finds the letter stuck in the billy when he goes to fetch the milk on Sunday morning. The billy lid is closed, and the note is in a sealed envelope. Robert Elliott gives it to Mrs Rhoda Grammar, who then gives it to another boy, Stanley Liddicoat, who had dropped by the house that morning, to take to the police.

The grubby scrap of paper is addressed to the manhunters of Ashhurst. It reads:

> To my fellow-men – After hearing a remark passed by one of the party this afternoon, to the effect that I am supposed to have burned down a house in town last night, I do hereby solemnly swear before my God Almighty that it is an untruth. At the time this man said the house was on fire – 9 p.m. he said – I was on the outskirts of Woodville. I might also state that a good many of the happenings of late that have been blamed on to me are false. I also heard P. Hanlon say while within one yard of me that I shot at my wife this morning. That also is a foul lie, and he went near getting a bullet for his pains. Excuse this writing, for I have only a pointed bullet to scrawl with. Signed, J. POWELKA, a man against the world.

The misspelling of the name Pawelka calls the authenticity of the note into question. But when the note gets produced as evidence at Pawelka's trial, the signature and handwriting are authenticated.

Pat Hanlon was Joe Pawelka's brother-in-law and Joe and Lizzie had been married in his home. According to newspaper reports, Hanlon had been living in fear of the fugitive ever since his escape. The fire referred to destroyed a two-story house in Palmerston on the night of Friday 8 April.

We can infer that 'last night' is 8 April, 'this morning' is 9 April when Joe tried to see Lizzie, and 'this afternoon' is the afternoon of the same day. In all likelihood, therefore, the note was placed in the billy under cover of darkness on the night of Saturday 9 April. The Grammars' house, on the main road to Palmerston, was isolated. Pawelka could have passed the gate on his way to town.

But Joe Pawelka's note is addressed to a community where he can expect little support. Eighty-five years later, informants would tell me that some Ashhurst people left food at their front gates at night for the fugitive, but almost everyone's allegiance is to Pawelka's wife and mother-in-law. Only in Kimbolton and the Pohangina Valley 'where he was well known, and where he was also liked' is there any sympathy for him. Yet he will not head home. He will return to the place where he is feared and despised, driven, it seems, by some imperative need to explain himself, to clear things up, and to win back his wife's affection.

◊

8

Shots in the Dark

The rain does not cease all day. After fleeing the Wilson house in Ashhurst, Joe Pawelka may have made his way up the Pohangina Valley and taken shelter in a haybarn. Then he may have come south across country, following Stoney Creek. More likely, he waited until after sunset at 5.30, returned to Ashhurst, left his note in the billy can, and walked toward Stoney Creek along the railway line.

The question is, did he then return to his hiding place on Stoney Creek or press on toward Palmerston in search of food and a raincoat?

Stoney Creek is a small Scandanavian settlement just east of Palmerston; today it is known as Whakarongo.

At 6.45 in the evening a man knocks on the door of the church and asks for a Mr Grover. The stranger is given directions to Grover's Store and post office next door. At the store, the stranger explains that he is a policeman engaged in the search for Pawelka. He stands out of the light as if not wanting to be recognised, and asks for an overcoat.

Three-quarters of an hour later, someone breaks into Amelia Farland's house at 128 Ferguson Street, Palmerston and steals two loaves of bread, 1 lb of butter, a tin of tea, 2 lbs of sugar, a billy can, a bottle of pickles and a green skull-cap. The key to the back door is also taken, and from a house opposite, an overcoat goes missing.

Was Joe Pawelka the man at Grover's Store who an hour later broke into Amelia Farland's house four miles away?*

It is possible that copycat criminals are at work. At Ashhurst, a young offender named Richard Collis has already exploited 'the Powelka pandemonium' by impersonating a special constable. He 'borrows' an overcoat, field glasses and money, and is given lodging for a week before clearing out with all his debts unpaid.

At 9.45 at 61 Ferguson Street, Leonard Hampton, master butcher and manager of Banks and Company's butchery in The Square, comes home from work on his bicycle to find a trip wire stretched across his driveway.

Leonard Hampton's house at 61 Ferguson Street.

Last year, Joe Pawelka worked at Banks' butchery for four months before Hampton sacked him because he 'found him such a liar'.

---

*   At his trial Pawelka is acquitted of the Farland burglary because of insufficient evidence.

Aware that Joe Pawelka knows that he always brings his takings home on Saturday nights, Hampton comes to the conclusion that Pawelka is seeking revenge. But when Hampton goes to the police, he is told that they are unable to send anyone to the house, and he returns home.

Searching his orchard the next day, Sunday 10 April, Hampton finds evidence that someone has camped there. Convinced that it must be Joe Pawelka, Hampton mounts vigil outside his house in the shadows of a willow and macrocarpa. At about 7 p.m., after a half-hour wait in darkness and rain, he hears the thud of someone jumping a fence. Then he sees a man cross the road, enter his driveway and latch the gate behind him.

In a sworn statement, Hampton – like Kendall on the previous Saturday – will claim to have positively identified the intruder, although he does not see his face and never gets close to him. 'The figure appeared to me [to be] Joseph Pawelka,' he will aver:

> That was the impression in my mind. He was wearing a three-quarter overcoat, a dark one .... It was the way he straightened himself up and walked across the road that made me think it was Pawelka. It was a pretty bad night at the time and it had just started to rain.

Hampton waits until the intruder has gone into the shadows, then runs to the police station. Six men are despatched immediately and quickly surround the house.

Police Sergeant McGuire and Detective Quartermain now approach the house from the front.

John Patrick Hackett McGuire has been in Palmerston only forty-eight hours, following a transfer from Lambton Quay, Wellington. Born and bred on the West Coast, he is forty-one and married with no children. But he is lacking in experience of practical policework, having served in Wellington as a clerk, his duties confined to 'quill driving'. He is unarmed. Quartermain is also from Wellington. *The New Zealand Truth* refers to him by his nickname, Demon, speaking scathingly of him as a city man, a fingerprint expert, with no experience of fieldwork or the bush. Unlike McGuire, Quartermain is armed.

In the pitch darkness, McGuire accosts and grapples with the intruder near Hampton's front door. The man is wearing a mask and a large hat. The two men wrestle their way across a gravel path to the front lawn where they tumble to the ground. The intruder stands up. A shot is fired. McGuire, lying on the ground, is hit in the stomach, just above the navel. He cries out, 'I'm hit!'

The track of the bullet is upward and to the left – a fact hard to reconcile with a shot being fired by someone standing over him.

Quartermain, who is 'but a short distance away', will later say he fired two shots toward 'the flash of Powelka's revolver', which gives rise to a rumour that it may have been he, not the intruder, who fatally wounded McGuire. Interviewed in hospital, McGuire says he 'could not actually say it was Powelka', and cannot say for certain whether he was shot by the intruder or by Quartermain.[*] Hampton, who supposed the intruder was his former employee, would not 'kiss the Bible to it' either.

As word of the shooting spreads, Palmerston is a 'maddened, frightened community' gripped by 'hysterical fever'. In the darkness and steady rain, old firearms – short-barrelled rifles, fowling-pieces, ancient revolvers – are requisitioned and handed out to civilian volunteers who form a cordon stretching a mile and a half around the Ferguson Street block. People cannot sleep. Shop owners leave their lights burning. Some hotels remain open all night. And reporters

---

[*] Sergeant McGuire, whose bullet wound caused irreversible liver damage and septic peritonitis, died at 6 a.m. on Thursday, 14 April. His funeral took place the following day at Pahiatua in torrential rain.

file their stories, declaring Pawelka to be a 'madman and thoroughly desperate', a 'criminal lunatic' who has 'terrorised a whole countryside'. 'The town is in a fearful state of excitement' one reporter writes. The cry is "Powelka! Powelka!" all day, 'and no one talks of anything else.' At Ashhurst 'the residents are in a great state of alarm.' Mrs Pawelka is said to be 'terrified'.

That night and the next morning, Pawelka is seen everywhere. He is sighted on the Rangitikei Line, near the flour mill, in North Street and at Awapuni. A woman in Terrace End reports a batch of scones and two loaves of bread taken by the fugitive. Concludes *The Manawatu Evening Standard*, 'these and other alarming rumours ... show that Powelka was hovering 'round Palmerston, and that something serious could be expected when night fell.'

But if Pawelka was the intruder at Hampton's house, he probably fled the scene of the shooting at once, cutting across paddocks toward the Manawatu River, using the cover of raupo swamps and lagoons in the Hokowhitu area. At his trial, however, Pawelka would vehemently deny having been anywhere near the scene of the crime, and during subsequent prison visits would protest his innocence, telling his family that he was in Tokomaru the night of the McGuire shooting, though he could not prove his alibi.

When McGuire is shot, an old schoolmate and close friend joins in the search for Pawelka. Michael (Mick) Quirk is a hairdresser amd tobacconist from Pahiatua, thirty-six and unmarried. His father and brother are both in the police force.

On the evening after the shooting of McGuire, Mick Quirk and another volunteer, Walter Henry Overton, are patrolling the streets of Palmerston. Overton is licensee of the Princess Hotel in Terrace End. He is thirty-five, an ex-artilleryman.

At 7.30 Overton is walking along a footpath at Terrace End with Sergeant Bowden from Feilding. Suddenly, out of the darkness they hear cries of 'Powelka! Powelka!' and see a man walking toward them with a revolver in his hand.

Overton and Bowden turn a powerful acetylene car headlight on the man, now fifteen yards away, and challenge him:

'Who are you?'

The man does not answer.

'Stop!'

There is no response.

'Stop or I'll fire!'

The man, dazzled by the glare from the lamp, stoops and lowers his head.

Overton fires, and the expanding bullet blows the back off Michael Quirk's head.

Overton, certain he has shot Pawelka, shouts, 'I've shot him, he's mine!'

Moments later, aware of his tragic mistake and realising that Quirk had not responded to his challenge because he probably thought Overton was the fugitive, Overton is 'stunned' and 'completely prostrated'.

At the inquest the next day, he appears 'broken up throughout the proceedings'.

Orders are now given to disarm and disband the vigilantes. At the same time the government doubles its reward to £100 for information leading to the capture of John Joseph Thomas Pawelka, described as having a large scar near his left shoulder blade, a scar on the side of his left kneecap, and pinched features. He is said to be wearing a dark grey coat, dark vest, greenish tweed trousers, a light well-worn shirt (torn in front), and blucher boots.

On the same evening, and at almost the same time Quirk is shot, a man with two revolvers accosts an old woman and child in Church Street. Ten minutes later, Alfred Richards, a farmer from Stoney Creek, is driving along East Street toward Ferguson Street when he is held at gunpoint by a man who then rummages in his cart for food. Richards has had dealings with Pawelka at the abattoirs and at butchers' shops. He is certain his assailant is Pawelka. Then, at Baldwin's Avenue, one street away from East Street, a Mr M.E. Leybourne, a commission agent, encounters a man with a revolver. When Leybourne asks the man if he is scouting for the fugitive, the man declares, 'I am Pawelka! Not another word or you are a dead man,' and presses the revolver to Leybourne's forehead before walking away.

In due course, the Leybourne stick-up will be shown to be the work of a prankster. But in Palmerston, the imagined now defines the real.

In truth, Pawelka was probably well away. At the time Quirk was shot and killed, Pawelka was positively identified by two constables twenty miles away as he approached the lower Gorge bridge from the direction of Woodville. This was about 7 p.m. When ordered to stand and put his hands up, he ignored the demand. He was again challenged before one of the constables fired two shots at him. The constable was convinced he had killed the fugitive, but next day it was found that the bullet had hit the woodwork of the bridge. It was supposed that Pawelka climbed over the side of the bridge and worked his way upstream under cover of darkness.

It is always in darkness that he is observed and identified.

Whatever the facts, this is the pattern now: every stranger at the door on a dark, rainy, windswept night will be Pawelka, and every case of burglary or arson will be blamed on him. Even allowing for the likelihood that copycat criminals are at work, newspapers will report that Pawelka has 'fired another unbalanced individual to emulation.'

The following day, Tuesday the 12th, Pawelka is again sighted, this time on the railway line near Bunnythorpe. It is three in the morning, the sighting is for less than a minute, and Constable Flannagan will report that Pawelka looked 'worn out and dejected.'

When Flannagan fired a shot, the man made off toward the Bunnythorpe School grounds, abandoning a swag containing both cooked and raw meat. A few hours later some pickles and dried fruit were stolen from a farmer's outhouse on the Ashhurst road half a mile away. And as day broke, another farmer, getting out his cows, surprised Pawelka lying on the ground.

Again it is a day of high winds and rain. In Palmerston, people feel 'it is absolutely unsafe for anyone to move about except in the most thickly trafficked places.' Excitement, according to the local newspaper, 'is rising to a great pitch'. As for Pawelka, the search for him goes on in falling temperatures, hurricane-force winds and driving rain. The general view is that he will head home to Kimbolton, travelling at night and sleeping by day, keeping to the Oroua River valley where there is bush cover. Several constables are stationed in the Kimbolton area; others scour the Oroua.

When he worked at the abattoirs, Joe had a reputation for great strength. He could lift a 300 lb side of beef with ease, or pick up two 90 lb carcasses, one in each hand. And people in Kimbolton often recounted how athletic he had been, how well he could jump. Now, however, Joe's mother is convinced that her son's health will not stand up to the ordeal of living rough and being on the run. She says, 'He will be found dead before the search continues much longer.'

In Kimbolton, a reporter finds the locals solidly in support of him. Small-town New Zealand is possessed of deep and parochial loyalties. While Ashhurst goes in fear of him and stands behind his estranged wife and in-laws, Kimbolton closes ranks to defend him.

'Those who know Powelka well say they have absolutely no fear of him, and do not believe he has fired on anybody,' one newspaperman reports. 'Everybody I spoke to ... seemed heartily sorry for Powelka, and all with whom he had dealings say that Powelka was a thoroughly upright fellow, one who could be trusted with anything. There seems to be no doubt in the minds of many people as to the author of the Palmerston shooting affray. Naturally the youth's parents are terribly cup [*sic*] up about the affair. They are old and respected residents of Kimbolton, and there seems little doubt that they would be glad to see Powelka captured, because he is evidently being blamed for many an ill deed that he has not committed.'

' "Everything is attributed to him," said a local resident yesterday, "and the statement was correct in every way." '

But many who know Pawelka take the view that he will not go home, but double back to Ashhurst and try again to see his wife. 'Rumour has it,' one newspaper reports with unintended poignancy, 'that Powelka is very much attached to his wife.'

9

Recaptured

I had reached a point in my research where I needed to see the places I'd been reading about and try to recapture in the landscape itself the mood of what had happened there. So I rented a car and headed north to the Manawatu.

As I approached Palmerston North, however, my preoccupation with Joe Pawelka gave way to memories of my own. As I slowed between the plane trees along Fitzherbert Avenue, I felt a tightening in my chest as though my body were registering things my consciousness could not yet grasp. I had lived nine years in this city surrounded by waterlogged paddocks, laid open to the lowering sky. A good half of my first marriage; the best years of my daughter's childhood. Now, coming back, I was thrown.

I had not expected this. I drove as in a dream, drawn toward the house where I had once lived.

The paint on the weatherboards and windowsills was peeling. The front porch was shaded by the native trees I had planted almost twenty years ago. In the driveway where my daughter once played, a little girl was sweeping the concrete with a yard broom. I felt I could have got out of the car and walked back into my previous existence.

I drove quickly away, passing through Terrace End – the same windswept and treeless avenue where Henry Overton shot Michael Quirk.

Downtown, I parked the car, put some coins in the meter, and drifted through the streets. Here was Thomas Cook's where I bought tickets to Africa and France. Here, H.L. Young Ltd – Stationers, Printers, Office Furnishers, Established 1901, where I bought typewriter ribbons. Coronation Building. Broadway Chambers. Tararua Workwear.

I went into Bennetts bookshop to find some of the maps and books I needed for my research. But when I asked an assistant if she had a copy of Stewart Lusk's history of Kimbolton, she said she didn't know.

'Can you find out for me?'

'Find out what?'

'Can't you check your computer and see if you have a copy in stock?'

'I don't think we have.'

'Could you just check?'

'What was it called?'

'I'm not sure of the title; the author is Stewart Lusk.'

'How do you spell that?'

'The surname is Lusk, L-U-S-K ....'

'Nothing under that name.'

'Are you sure?'

'I told you we didn't have it.'

I went back to the car. In the distance, the backbone of the Ruahines was a smudge of dark green under a colourless sky.

It was now the middle of the afternoon. The light was failing. There were dark stands of macrocarpas in the paddocks, and a band of white light over the range, as in one of McCahon's canvases. North, overnight, snow had dusted the peaks of the Ruahines. In the south, sunlight flooded the plain, momentarily touching the domes and hillocks of the Tararua foothills.

At Ashhurst, I found the site of the Wilson house on the corner of Salisbury and Wyndham Streets. There was nothing to see, nothing to give the imagination purchase or provide a link to the lives of those who once lived there.

I turned the car and drove slowly back to the centre of town, reliant now solely on my research notes to reconstruct the events that unfolded in the stormy darkness of 17 April 1910.

For five days the search for Pawelka is hindered by equinoctial gales and heavy rain, and the fugitive lies low, probably in the Longburn area where 6 lb of steak and 4 lb of German sausage are stolen from the Manawatu Meat Company's shop on Friday the 15th. A sou'wester hat and oilskin coat are also taken from the butcher's house. Almost certainly Joe Pawelka travels from Longburn to Palmerston on Saturday afternoon, buying 3 lb of his favourite cream crackers, 1 lb of cheese and 4 pennyworth of matches from Cox's store in Ferguson Street before heading yet again toward Ashhurst. The rain has not let up.

A reporter in *The New Zealand Times* writes of this irrational refusal to escape from the region where he is hunted. Why is he compelled to return over and over again to the very place where he is most likely to be caught? The reporter can only suggest 'a deranged mind.'

It is the coldest night of the year. In Ashhurst, in windswept darkness before dawn on Sunday 17 April, one policeman has Mrs Wilson's house under surveillance; two others are watching Pat Hanlon's house; two are patrolling the town.

The policemen outside Hanlon's house in Winchester Street are hidden in the shadows of a macrocarpa hedge. Constable John J. Gallagher is from Wellington. He had been responsible for security at the lock-up in Lambton Quay when Pawelka escaped on 23 March, and is determined to repair his damaged reputation. His companion is a Probationer called Callery.

At 4 a.m., in torrential rain, Gallagher and Callery see a man cross a side street and head toward Hanlon's paddock. When they call on him to stop, he dives over a fence (they hear the ting of the fencing wire), dropping some water biscuits and bottles of stout. Callery fires a shot after the fleeing man.

Gallagher reports the sighting to the constables on patrol who then notify Constable Thompson at the Wilson house.

Because the man was seen coming from the direction of Scott's farm (about a quarter of a mile from the post office), and could have easily doubled back there after diving over Hanlon's fence, the police decide to search the farm buildings.

It is now 6.30 a.m. Watts and Thompson inspect the cowshed. Thompson checks the hayloft. Then, joined by two civilian searchers, they move on to the neighbouring farm.

Currie's cowshed is across the road from the Grammars' house where Pawelka left his note, written with the lead of a bullet, signed 'a man against the world'. The cowshed is a large weatherboard building with eleven bails on either side of a central aisle. The aisle is uncovered and open at either end. Above the bails are haylofts.

Thompson takes the loft on the left. Gallagher takes the one on the right, using a haycart to clamber up. The other searchers remain below.

Thompson finds nothing and calls across to Gallagher, 'Do you see anything?'

Gallagher can't see much in the bad light and strikes a match. He discerns a man lying full length between the loft wall and a heap of hay. The man has a revolver in his hand; an empty bottle of stout lies nearby. With considerable sang-froid, Gallagher shouts down to the others, 'There is no one here.'

Gallagher descends into the yard, holding up his hand to caution silence.

While the searchers work out their plan of attack, a railway clerk named Bryce is sent to fetch an acetylene bicycle lamp.

When everything is ready, Callery and the second civilian searcher, Sheridan, remain below. Sylvester and Watts take one end of the loft, while Gallagher and Thompson take the other. Thompson has the lamp. He turns it on Pawelka as he and Gallagher rush forward. Pawelka raises his revolver, but Thompson knocks his hand up into the air and disarms him. There is a short struggle as Pawelka is handcuffed. Then he is helped down from the loft.

As the party set off toward the Ashhurst police station, Pawelka mutters, 'You bloody cowards!' He walks in a shuffle, making some of his guards think he might be drunk. Once he tries to trip Gallagher and struggles to get away. 'Do you think I'm a coward?' he says, and, indicating his handcuffs, adds, 'If so, take these off, and I'll show you.'

'It's all right, Joe,' Gallagher says. 'You wouldn't shoot a man.'

Thompson then says, 'No? Who shot poor McGuire?'

Pawelka allegedly turns his head to Thompson and asks, 'Who fired the first shot, you bastards?' But at his trial, Pawelka will declare angrily that this is a police lie.

At the police station he is searched. Apart from the two revolvers in his possession when captured at Currie's cowshed (a .32 and a .380 Harrington), he has ammunition, eight detonators, several pennies, eight threepenny bits, four candles of various lengths, a sock, a new but soiled shirt with a Millar and Giorgi label, a chisel, some notepaper, a copy of Saturday night's *Manawatu Evening Standard*, a couple of postal notes and 18 penny stamps. Most telling, when one considers that he has been captured in the town to which his affections have doomed him to return so many times, is the discovery of a photo of his wife and his mother-in-law in his pocket.

The police recognise the postal notes, stamps and stout as stolen from the Ashhurst railway station where there'd also been a failed attempt to blow the safe earlier in the night.

Pawelka's captors are surprised that the fugitive does not look like a man who has been on the lam and living rough for twenty-four days. He is clean-shaven except for a small moustache and his hair is combed. He is wearing the sou'wester hat and black oilskin coat stolen from Longburn the previous day over a grey three-quarter coat. Under the coat he has an ordinary suit of clothes, one sock (the other is in his pocket), and his now-famous green riding pants and yellow leggings. There is no evidence on his leggings or clothing that he has been wading rivers.

Had he made himself presentable before yet another bid to see his wife?

Whatever his appearance, he is a man in despair.

'This is hell upon earth,' he says to his captors. 'Why didn't you put a bullet into me? Put one now and they will think I did it myself. I wanted to see my wife, and then I would have put a bullet into myself. She is an affectionate wife. My wife has led me to this. My heart is broken. I can feel nothing.'

At about 9 in the morning, the prisoner is taken to Palmerston by car. Once he struggles to throw himself from it, as if the impulse to escape now blurs with the impulse to do away with himself. At Palmerston he is stripped and given hot coffee and blankets. In his cell he collapses and weeps, but most of the time he paces up and down and asks for his wife, 'speaking affectionately of her'. He is told she will not come. He does not sleep, but stands all day at the cell door looking out through the spy hole. He blames a Shannon man called Archie McRae for all his troubles, alleging that McRae sold him the stolen furniture which was found in his Church Street house.

When a local doctor visits him and offers him a sleeping draught to calm his nerves, Pawelka asks that he be given poison instead 'to finish himself off'.

Twenty-four hours after being recaptured, Pawelka begins his journey back to Wellington. Handcuffed to Gallagher and Callery, and escorted by several constables returning to the capital, Pawelka sits in a second-class carriage with the blinds drawn. Already he has been charged with the murder of McGuire. Other charges are pending.

In Wellington he is arraigned in the Magistrate's Court. His appearance now gives away his state of mind. His hair is dishevelled. His collar is turned up for warmth. One newspaper reporter writes that the prisoner's eyes wandered restlessly and uneasily around the room, that he looked 'fatigued, as if he had had quite enough.'

He is charged with breaking and entering Dixon's butchery on or about 6 August 1909 and stealing a butcher's steel valued at ten shillings. The trial date is set for 26 April and he is remanded in custody.

Pawelka tells his counsel that he is not guilty of murder. He repeats his story about McRae being the cause of all his troubles. He declares that the only thing he is sorry for is that he did not shoot McRae, and that if ever he got out again he would.

ᚼᚼ

10

No Quarter

As I drove north, the light drained from the sky and the darkness came up out of the land. I felt I was travelling not through space, but time. I drove through country towns where mud-splattered utes were parked against the kerb, and groups of disgruntled young men dressed in shapeless clothing stood and stared. I drove down a highway where white crosses and wreaths marked the site of fatal accidents.

Toward midnight, on the volcanic plateau, the sky began to clear and the moon came out.

The mountains were like great mounds of rock salt.

At Waiouru, I stopped at a diner and ordered black coffee and a couple of doughnuts. A radio was playing hits from the '70s, and the announcer was promoting a film called *True Lies*.

In the beginning, Joe claimed that he was not guilty of the furniture thefts that had been 'the cause of all his troubles'. When arrested in February 1910, he protested that he'd bought the furniture from Archie McRae in good faith, unaware he was receiving stolen goods. When recaptured after the manhunt in April 1910, he repeated this story and blamed Archie McCrae for selling him stolen property. Indeed, his anger at his erstwhile mate was so intense that he said he would shoot him if he got the chance. A year later, however, in a letter written to Lizzie from prison, Joe would assert that he was not 'solely responsible for stealing the furniture', implying that he *had* been guilty. Then, as if determined to make the most of this confession and appear praiseworthy in her eyes, he added that he had *not* divulged McCrae's name to the police because his accomplice was married and had two children.

These shifting stories suggest that for Joe Pawelka truth was simply the most expedient lie.

But the thing about inveterate liars is the difficulty they have remembering their lies. This is their fatal flaw: sooner or later, they incriminate themselves through inconsistency. But they also reveal themselves. So we learn the truth about Joe Pawelka in his lies: his desperate need for approval and affection; his vilification of those who did not mirror him, who failed to meet his overweening needs. This is why, even as he sought to win back his wife, he made threats against her and cursed her for abandoning him.

Given his desperation, it is difficult to judge him. When one thinks of all the crimes against humanity that have been done in the name of Truth, one wonders if the consequences of mendacity and deceit have been any more terrible.

In any event, what one person will call a lie, another will deem a truth.

Perhaps what matters is not the words, but whether the words sustain us, and help us survive.

I drove all night and reached Auckland before dawn. My father opened the front door to me. He was in his dressing gown.

His anxious face broke into a smile. 'I wasn't expecting you until Sunday.'

'I drove all night.'

'I thought you weren't coming 'til Sunday.'

'Sorry if I dragged you out of bed. I thought you'd be up.'

'I let myself sleep in a bit these days. Not much point now getting up with the lark.'

I followed him through to the kitchen where he put the kettle on and asked if I would like some breakfast.

It grieved me to see how frail he was, how unsteady on his feet.

When my mother died, he amazed everyone with his resolve 'to get out and about again'. But whenever I phoned him long-distance, he would talk at length about some new illness that had undermined his confidence and made him as housebound as he had been during the last two years of my mother's life. Now it was attacks of vertigo which destabilised and defeated him.

'I can't understand it,' he said. 'And the doctor doesn't seem to be able to work out what the dings it is.'

But he wasn't going to give in to it. He was determined to play croquet again. He practised every day, hitting balls along the hall carpet. The trouble was he could hit a ball accurately indoors, but out on the croquet lawn, in the open air, he failed to hit anything.

'I don't know what I'm doing wrong. It hurts me like mad.'

We sat at the dining table as dawn broke.

'But I'm persisting. It'll come right. It's only a matter of practice. It'll get better bit by bit.'

I knew it would not get better. I knew that he could not play croquet because my mother was not there to play with him. And his loneliness was all the more heartbreaking because he denied it.

When my father went to get dressed, I told him I would try to catch a couple of hours sleep. Then we could talk some more.

But he could not let me go. He needed to talk. He kept turning to the chocolate boxes on the table, filled with old photos and letters.

'I don't know if I ever showed you this,' he said. 'I don't know whether you've ever seen this.'

Of course, I had seen them all.

He kept returning to his youth. The friends he had back then. The things they did. He told me about the day he and a couple of friends spent at a river hole outside Moabite. When it came time to head for home, they decided to walk back across country rather than thumb a ride on the main road. They walked in the rain for five hours. It was seven in the evening when they got back. My father went straight to the Coffee Palace where he was staying and fell asleep. He forgot that he had arranged to meet his fiancée at 7.30.

'Another time, Bob Street, Vern Devereux and I climbed the mountain from the North Egmont House to see the sun rise. We thought we'd missed it, because the sky began to lighten before we reached the summit. But the summit was in cloud, so we had a clear view after all, and we watched the sun come up over Ngaruahoe and Tongariro away to the east. I took that photo.'

'Did I ever show it to you? I used that old box brownie I gave you.'

'Yes,' I said, remembering the mountains as I had seen them in the moonlight ten hours before and recalling old sepia snapshots of my father standing on a rocky spur, ice axe in hand, or lying on a scree slope with his friends.

After a couple of hours sleep, I rejoined my father. He was playing his harmonica. The songs went back to the period after World War I when he was growing up. My bonnie lies over the ocean ... John Brown's body ... Pack up your troubles ... My darling Clementine ... There's no place like home ... Keep the home fires burning ...

The maudlin tunes depressed me. I suggested we go out for a while. Perhaps we could walk up to the local shops. I needed to buy some coffee.

'That's a good idea,' my father said.

'Maybe later we could go downtown.'

It took us half an hour to walk the two blocks to the shops. Crossing the road was a nightmare.

But it cheered my father up and he was eager now to have me drive him into the city. He wanted to go to a couple of second-hand bookshops and look for old books about Taranaki.

'When I'm here on my own,' he said, 'I don't seem to be able to get up much interest in anything.'

'I know how you feel. I've been through it too.'

'It's hard to cook meals for yourself. It's hard to get up much of an appetite when you're eating on your own.'

On the way into the city, I tried to talk to him about grief. I wanted him to know that he was not alone in his pain. That everyone suffered bereavement in much the same way. It was like the bond between parent and child: one of the things we all share, no matter who we are, what we believe, what society we grow up in.

I told him about Joe Pawelka. I mentioned the traumatic lung operation he'd undergone, how it had sapped his strength and left him with a strange hiss in his voice. I told him how Joe got married, only to have his wife walk out on him after two months. I recounted his losses.

'I think a lot of his anger was a protest against loss. A sense of cosmic unfairness. Why me? Why now? And this sense of loss must have been made worse because of his sense of social inferiority. His wife's family looked down on him and made him feel inadequate. Yet the strange thing was that after he was recaptured he never said a word against her, but kept affirming what an affectionate woman she was ....'

'When I met Emily, her parents thought I wasn't good enough for her,' my father said. 'It's funny, but it's a fact ... sometimes now I wonder what she saw in me.'

On 29 April 1910, twelve days after his arrest, Joe Pawelka is taken to Palmerston for trial.

A large crowd is at the station to meet the Wellington train. Pawelka, manacled and escorted by police, appears fit and well. He is wearing a soft white shirt and green tie. As he is led away, someone calls from the crowd, 'You're a hero, Pawelka,' and the hero smiles.

Later, entering the packed courtroom handcuffed to his captors, Gallagher and Callery, he appears confident and even defiant, walking 'almost majestically' to the dock.

As the thirteen indictments are read, a chain is forged from the theft of the butcher's steel on 13 July 1909 to the fires in Palmerston on the night of 5 April.

The trial sessions continue into June. Proceedings are reported in detail by the press. Millar and Giorgi, making the most of the free publicity, run half-page advertisements in the *Manawatu Evening Standard* for a 'Great Sale of Salvaged Stock' from the fire which Joe Pawelka is accused of starting. Between court hearings, Pawelka is returned, heavily manacled, to Wellington's Terrace prison.

At each of his appearances in court he listens carefully, smiling when an absurd charge is read, and occasionally asking for pencil and paper so he can take notes. On 6 May, when charged with the murder of Sergeant McGuire he gives a 'convulsive start', but pleads not guilty in 'a clear voice, sharp and emphatic'.

It is not until 30 May that the evidence has been heard and reviewed. In his summing up, Mr Justice Cooper points out that in the case of the McGuire shooting the evidence is circumstantial. Ominously, however, he compares it to a rope, 'each strand of which, though not strong enough to stand alone, yet contributed to the strength of the whole.'

When the jury comes in, a hush falls over the courtroom. Joe Pawelka, 'labouring under great excitement', eagerly scans their faces.

There is reasonable doubt. He is found 'not guilty' of murder.

But the tension of the trial has brought him to the limits of his endurance and he is taken from the courtroom in a state of collapse.

When the trial resumes on 1 June, Pawelka is obviously distressed. He demands of the police that he be permitted to appear before the court in his dress suit. The request is refused on the grounds that the suit was stolen. In court he looks 'worn and weary'. His manner is described as 'peculiar'. The police suggest he is 'shamming' and 'feigning insanity'.

To the ten charges of breaking and entering, theft and escape from custody, he pleads guilty. To the charges of arson he pleads not guilty, even though he was captured in clothing stolen from Millar and Giorgi's draper's shop, and his fingerprints were found on broken glass from the burned-down high school. Evidence that Pawelka was guilty of robbery under arms (the Kendall hold-up) is considered too flimsy to sustain an indictment.

The trial ends on 5 June, five weeks after it began. Three days later, Pawelka comes up for sentencing.

He stands before the court neatly dressed and clean-shaven.

Asked if he has anything to say before sentencing, he declares: 'I am very sorry for the offences I have committed, and for which I appear before the Court. I hope you will be as lenient as possible with me. I committed some of the offences because I had to exist. Although I was found guilty of the furniture stealing, I no more stole the furniture than you did, sir!'

'Then you should not have pleaded guilty,' Justice Cooper replies.

'I couldn't do anything else. The man I bought it off could not be found. I had receipts for it, but they could not be found either.'

At this moment Pawelka falls back in a faint, and a glass of water is brought for him.

He drinks, then in an almost inaudible voice attempts to tell his story. 'I have had a very hard life, and have practically been on my own since I was thirteen years old. As for the charge of murder, I –'

'You were acquitted of that.'

'I know, but people say I'm still guilty. I swear I was never near the place. I would sooner hang than be thought guilty.'

With nothing more to say, Pawelka waits while Justice Cooper prepares his remarks.

'It is a very painful thing to have to pass sentence on a man as young as you are for a series of very serious crimes. But I have to do my duty. I have to protect the public against such offences. It may be that your early life has had something to do with your relapse into crime, but you have certainly during the past twelve months committed as many crimes (I am only referring to those crimes to which you have pleaded guilty and of which you were found guilty) as an ordinary criminal commits in the whole course of his life. You commenced your career of crime on the first November with the theft of a bicycle, and followed it by a series of offences of the most serious description – breaking and entering and stealing goods from the houses of various persons in this district. You have pleaded guilty in all to seven charges of breaking and entering from December last until February this year before your first escape from custody. On twelfth March you escaped. Then came another series of offences committed by you. You have pleaded guilty to five more charges of breaking and entering and have been found guilty of arson. I have a report which indicates that no doubt you have an ill-balanced mind. You attempted suicide before your first arrest. I have to do what I can to protect you against yourself, and I have to do more. I have to protect the public against you.'

As the sentences are handed down, Pawelka seems stunned. When he hears the first sentence of seven years, he groans. He receives the second and third in silence. After pronouncing a cumulative sentence of twenty-one years, Mr Justice Cooper observes that Pawelka is an habitual criminal, implying the possibility of indefinite detention.

Even before the sentence, sympathy for Pawelka had been growing. On the day Joe Pawelka was recaptured, *The New Zealand Truth* observed that he had already been 'condemned without trial', and there was every possibility that some 'mad-headed civilian or reward-seeking policeman might obviate the necessity of placing him in the dock'. The conduct of the manhunt also came in for criticism. *The Christchurch Press* compared it to a hunt for a mad dog which would have driven any man to deeds of violence. Now, with the sentence passed, *The New Zealand Times* reproached the judge, calling the heavy sentence worse than a death sentence, 'a clumsy attempt to wreak vengeance on a half-demented offender'. One contemporary observer wrote: 'Never in the history of New Zealand has there been such an agitation as that which followed the sentencing of Pawelka.'

Dozens of letters to newspapers called the sentence cruel and inhuman. Protest meetings were held and trade unions took up the case. Delegations to the Minister of Justice asked that the sentence be reduced to fourteen years. Only *The Manawatu Evening Standard*, speaking on behalf of the region which had borne the brunt of the manhunt, declared the sentence fair. In an editorial of 10 June, one reads: 'There is certainly a very humane and growing tendency to regard moral perversion more in the light of a disease and to prescribe reformative treatment rather than retributive punishment, but until the principle is completely recognised, judges have merely to administer the law as they find it.'

Even in the Manawatu, not everyone shared this view. Pawelka committees were formed in Palmerston and Wanganui to press for a reduction in the sentence. And two men were brought before the court in Palmerston for coming to blows over the question as to whether Pawelka was rightly or wrongly treated.

All this was symptomatic of a deep division in New Zealand at the time. The poor who migrated to New Zealand in the late nineteenth century had hoped for freedom from want and from exploitation. But in the early 1890s, with the economy coming slowly out of recession, the gap between workers and the well-to-do was widening. At one extreme were bankers, merchants, manufacturers, run-holders and wealthy farmers with their chambers of commerce, Agricultural and Pastoral Associations and élite social clubs. At the other extreme was an underclass struggling for living wages, bearable hours and decent working conditions. Between these extremes was a burgeoning white-collar society of small businessmen, clerks, doctors, lawyers, and self-employed tradesmen whose values and aspirations were, by and large, those of the rich, not the poor. For a while, the poor saw unionisation as an answer, and in 1891 trade union membership rose to a peak of about twenty-three per cent of the population. The destitute and poor also made their voices heard in less legitimate protests: street marches in the cities, and, in rural areas, sheep stealing and rick and barn burning.

By 1910, when Pawelka was tried and sentenced, trade unions were strong. A successful strike by miners at Blackball in 1908 had inspired watersiders, shearers, labourers and clothing workers to consider 'direct' action in the 'class war' and members of these labour organisations saw Joe Pawelka as a victim of the class whose slogans about law and order disguised a double standard. The wealthy and educated got justice; the poor and uneducated lost out.

Thus Joe Pawelka became New Zealand's first avatar of that mythical figure whom John Mulgan called Man Alone – a man of the working class, a bushman, a rugged individualist, an underdog, a law unto himself. We would recognise him again in 1941 when the Kowhitirangi farmer, Eric Stanley Graham, ran amok, and in 1962 when George Wilder broke out of New Plymouth Gaol and went bush.

But though poverty and powerlessness may have been the soil in which the seeds of Joe Pawelka's discontent took root, it would be a mistake to reduce the meaning of his life to that stony ground where he was born and raised.

Joe Pawelka abhorred cowardice, was driven by a need to prove himself the equal of any man, and had a bone to pick with the world. As a boy he fashioned a revolver from a sawn-off .22 rifle and became a crack shot. At one time he thought of becoming a policeman or railway guard. He was an avid reader of such penny dreadfuls as Deadwood Dick. He felt lonely, abandoned, hard done by and thwarted in his ambitions. But such dreams and adversities have been shared by thousands who did not share his fate.

It is the particular way in which Joe Pawelka *lived* his fate that I find fascinating. The question of how a person acts when robbed of the power to act.

'We are not lumps of clay,' Sartre writes in his biography of Jean Genet, 'and what is important is not what people make of us but what we ourselves make of what they have made us.'

Was there a lesson to be learned from Genet who, when deprived of *his* freedom and made a scapegoat for the anxieties of others, embraced this lack of freedom as though he himself had willed it – deciding, as he put it, *'to be what crime had made of me – a thief'*?

That night I could not sleep for thinking about Moabite and my life growing up there.

For most of his working life my father had been a clerk in the Bank of New South Wales. With five children, my parents had struggled to 'make ends meet'. Yet though we were poor and lived among the poor, my parents' social world was the educated middle-class. My father played golf every weekend with bank managers, store owners, accountants, solicitors and doctors; my mother played bridge and mah-jong with their wives.

My father was a shy man, with little ambition or bravado. And he did not drink. In his social circle, he was alone in being unable to afford a motor car. Every Saturday morning, he would ring around for a lift to the golf club. I always saw this as a humiliating thing for him to have to do. Sometimes he would tell my mother he couldn't be bothered phoning, and would set off on foot with his battered golf bag and antique clubs, wearing plus-fours, hoping to be picked up by someone along the highway. But he would walk without looking back, not deigning to thumb a ride.

From the time I was ten, I accompanied him to the links every weekend to scour ditches, gullies, river holes and barberry hedges for lost golf balls which I would sell for sixpence each. With this pocket money, I saved up for such things as a microscope and camera.

As I remember it, the worst moments for my father were when he came into the clubhouse – the nineteenth hole – at the end of a drab winter's afternoon. His scorecard would be filled with double and triple bogeys, frustrating his hopes of ever reducing his handicap. And he would be mocked for his refusal to have a drink.

'Come on D'arcy, one for the road.'

'How about a shandy!'

'A triple shandy!'

He had no response to this raillery. We would leave the golf club together in silence and cross the railway line onto the main road.

All my life the self-congratulatory braggadocio of the good citizen has left me cold. In a way, I internalised and dramatised my father's plight. I imagined that the only way I could endure my own sense of inferiority was to pre-empt it. To actively reject the very society I imagined to have rejected me. I did not despise my father for his failings. They mirrored my own. But as my scorn for the bourgeoisie grew stronger, so did my identification for those I saw as its victims.

This affinity for those on the wrong side of the tracks is a habit I cannot break.

Perhaps my father felt the same way after all his years in the bank. His mother was a snob who pushed her son into a white-collar job 'for his own good', assuring him it would guarantee security. The truth is she did not want him to follow his father's trade and become a carpenter.

I once asked my father what had been his best years in the bank. He said 'Nelson'. This was the city where he and my mother started out and where their first two children were born.

He became a self-taught expert in import licensing. But then he was moved to Taranaki where there was no call for this expertise. As he told it, his working life was a series of such set-backs.

'When the wool boom began in the fifties I developed a system for banking wool cheques, but I couldn't get anyone at head office interested, so my scheme was just filed away and ignored. Then, years later, after I'd lost all interest, the bank dusted it off and adopted it as standard banking policy.'

It was always the same. He would 'swot up' on some subject, create a 'system' or 'scheme', only to encounter indifference or derision.

'Goodness knows why. I've never been able to fathom it.'

But I knew why. I knew that my father inspired no respect among the people with whom he worked. Whenever he got onto his favourite subject of efficiency in the workplace and suggested some initiative for cutting costs or saving money, people laughed at him. His consolation became his family. He repaired to his workshop and made wooden toys for his children. Or built wireless transmitters and talked to radio hams all over the world, exchanging technical data, call signs and frequencies – things that would not take him out of his depth.

He quit the bank when he was fifty-five and took a succession of jobs with import firms and small businesses around Auckland. As a superannuitant, he was assigned only menial jobs. He worked for a customs clearing agency, a cloth importer, a paper merchant. Still he came up with ideas to improve efficiency. As usual, he was knocked back. One supervisor asked him how one could clear cheques in quick time and my father worked out a system. 'That wouldn't work!' he was told. In the end he began to mark time until he was sixty-five and could retire. He was so switched off that he used to fall asleep on the job or forget to finish the work he had been told to do.

'At one job, the central heating in the lunch room made me nod off while I was eating my sandwiches. When I woke up I was five minutes late in getting back to my desk. They sacked me. The next job, I avoided the lunch room and took to eating my lunch in the basement with the storemen. I got on with them famously. But the clerks in the lunch room wouldn't have anything to do with me.'

One of his last jobs was at the Reserve Bank. Glass partitions enabled the supervisors to monitor the clerks. My father would wave and smile at the overseers, trying to break down their stern and self-important facades. Once again he got the sack.

It was only after he retired that he came into his own. He took up carpentry again – the trade he would have followed had it not been for his mother's prejudice and ambition. He set up a studio-workshop and made frames for my mother's paintings. They worked beside each other. They played croquet together. In the evenings, they watched their favourite TV programmes. They were as at home in each other's company as it is possible for two human beings to be.

I let myself out of the house as quietly as I could and walked away. There was a wan street light on the corner. Elsewhere it was pitch dark. The suburb where my parents created their haven had always been, for me, a wilderness. In its empty streets my worst fears were realised. Of the loss of community. Of loss of contact with the world. I remembered the nights in Moabite when I walked to the town library in the dark. Heavy swing doors led into the Municipal Chambers. Then a long corridor hung with photos of Moabite as it had been in the beginning: a smoke-obscured clearing, a wall of unfelled bush, huts surrounded by rough fences, a litter of splintered logs, and muddy tracks. The library was a place of light and warmth. Shelves of new books from the Country Library Service would transport me into another world, steeling me for the long walk home when a train whistle in the hills was the promise of another life, but a morepork forlorn in the darkness taught me to count on nothing.

☙❧

11

Escape

Joe Pawelka was sentenced in early June 1910. Six weeks later his daughter was born in Ashhurst. Lizzie, who had reverted to her maiden name, christened the child Iris. Father and daughter would never see each other, and for two generations the Wilsons would expunge the name Pawelka from their lives.

Joe Pawelka was held in a condemned cell at Wellington's Terrace Gaol and kept under constant surveillance. It was intended that he should move to a new wing of the prison as soon as construction was complete.

His family came to see him often. Joe always complained that Lizzie had not got in touch with him and would ask when he was going to have a chance to see his daughter. Louisa, who had visited the Wilsons in Ashhurst on several occasions, knew Lizzie would never consent to see Joe. And Lizzie refused to allow him to see Iris either.

For a while Joe feigned sickness. Then he seemed to reconcile himself to his fate and accept the constraints of prison life.

Iris as a small child.

Indeed, it seems that he immediately set out to win the hearts of those guarding him. He gave no trouble, was docile and conformed to prison discipline, and in fact, became a model prisoner.

Escape seems to have been the last thing possible, and, to the official mind, escape was impossible. The strict watch of the day and night was relaxed and as Pawelka made splendid progress physically, actually benefiting by the regular hours of gaol life, it was deemed necessary that the prisoner should learn a trade – tailoring or boot-making. Pawelka chose the latter. The result was that the prisoner now mingled more freely with his fellow inmates, and from their daily intercourse Pawelka began to be regarded in the light of a hero. Every prisoner was a sympathiser and wished Pawelka all sorts of luck. The eastern wing was completed, and in due course Pawelka shifted his quarters from the condemned cell. He was an omnivorous reader of light fiction, and his vice of cigarette smoking was indulged him. Even his gaolers sympathised with him because of the term of imprisonment he had to serve.

But a fortnight after the birth of his daughter, Joe Pawelka revealed his hidden hand.

A twelve or fourteen-foot double galvanised iron fence had been erected around the new wing. With the help of another prisoner, Joe slipped into the space between the two fences and waited for nightfall. Unfortunately for him, his absence from the boot shop was noticed almost at once and he was found and returned to his cell.

A week later he tried again to break out. Using a hacksaw blade, he sawed through the one-inch iron bars that protected his eighteen-inch cell window. It was only by chance that a warder caught him in the act of wriggling out. His cell was searched and several more hacksaw blades were found (of a type used in the prison workshop), together with a rope ladder and a suit of black street clothes, presumably smuggled in by one of his prison visitors.

He was now watched both night and day and denied all privileges. Undeterred, he attempted his third escape three days later.

On 17 August, the criminal court was in session and several of Pawelka's gaolers had to attend. That day Pawelka was placed in a small triangular yard, supervised by an armed warder in a watchtower. A moment's inattention was all he needed. He leaped onto a ledge – a blind spot beneath the watchtower – scrambled over a corrugated iron roof and dropped into the street. Again luck was against him.

The wife of an ex-gaoler spotted his arrow-marked prison uniform and raised the alarm. A quarter-hour after his escape he was found hiding under a cottage in Woolcombe Street not far from the gaol.

He was placed in a condemned cell again and a light kept burning at night. There were two fifteen-by-twelve-inch gratings to this cell, each covered by a shutter. The shutters allowed warders to observe him at any time, and instructions were posted that Pawelka was to be checked every fifteen minutes.

The two condemned cells were in poor repair. Indeed, in Pawelka's cell one of the barred observation windows could not be locked. Before first light on Sunday 27 August, Joe removed one of the windows from its frame, got out into the corridor leading to the gaol office and crossed into the kitchen yard. There he scaled a wall, clambered across the kitchen roof and dropped eight feet onto a small hill outside the prison overlooking the Terrace.

The escape was well-timed. It was Sunday. It was dark. And it was pouring with rain.

Pawelka had waited until an orderly officer checked his cell at 6 o'clock before making his move. But his escape would have been impossible without complicity. The screws that held the window in its frame had been removed by inmates during a renovation of the cell block three or four months before. When the prison workers reinstalled the window they embedded it in blanket fluff and clay, and created dummy screws with paint and putty. Also in Pawelka's favour, the door to the kitchen yard had been opened at 4.45 a.m. to allow the prison cooks access to the kitchen. Possibly another door leading from the corridor outside Pawelka's cell to the single officer's quarters had also been left open when the officer's cook passed through with a cup of tea for the chief warder.

Warder Eric Wallace raised the alarm a few minutes after 6 a.m. After checking the prisoner, he had gone to padlock a gate to the penal yard. But hearing a 'sharp noise', he had retraced his steps.*

Pawelka was gone.

His shoes were outside the cell door. Inside the cell were his arrow-marked cap and blankets, together with some cigarette butts and three books: *Pickwick Papers, America at Work,* and *No Name.*

The day broke wet and windy. Sixty police were brought in for the search. They scoured the Wellington hills, searched houses, trampled gardens, kept a watch on the waterfront and set up roadblocks on the main roads out of the city, but apart from a single report by a milk-delivery boy who said he'd seen a figure in white making for the Botanical Gardens before dawn, there were no sightings, no clues.

In the weeks that followed there was talk of Pawelka being taken aboard a schooner bound for Australia, of Pawelka drowning in Wellington Harbour, and of Pawelka being given his freedom when he agreed, in the absence of the official hangman, to execute a condemned Maori murderer called Kaka.

Rumour and rain covered his tracks.

෴

---

* The following month, though absolved from 'wilful neglect', Warder Wallace was dismissed from the prison service.

The Blind Impress

II

THE BLIND IMPRESS

12

Starting Over

Just north of Mangaweka, I turned off the main highway. The road went down toward the river. The water was turquoise, exposed papa clay of the bluffs glistening with sweat. Crossing the Rangitikei, the bridge boards clonked and rumbled under the car.

The road was like wire from a caisson – curled. It twisted and turned through small valleys. Stones knocked against the floor of the car. My tyres slipped on the loose metal. Dust churned up behind.

Every now and then I glimpsed the Ruahines, cloud shadows moving slowly over the range.

I passed sheep sheds with roofs of faded red oxide. Sheep pens and holding paddocks. Hillsides were overrun with rushes or dead thistles.

I could smell scorched grass in the wind.

Henry had written me instructions on how to find his house. But I wanted to make the most of the day before arriving there, so had chosen the back country roads to Rangiwahia before turning south toward Utuwai. Once on the Pohangina Valley East Road I was to look out for a red barn, then take a stony track up into the hills for about two miles. Henry had said 'You can't miss it.'

By the time I parked the rental car at the end of the track I was sure I *had* missed it. But I pulled my grip from the car and started through the manuka scrub toward what looked like a house.

I felt uneasy – still shaken by my father's death which had brought me home again and troubled that nine years had passed since I'd last seen Henry and Karen. I wished I had looked them up when I'd been in New Zealand eight months ago, doing my first stint of research.

The house was built on poles, a makeshift structure with creosoted weatherboarding, windows from a demolished schoolhouse, a chimney of hammered tin. Ferns flourished in the dank shadows under a broad deck.

I climbed the river-stone steps to the deck and peered into the house. There was a woman sitting at the table. I did not want to startle her, so knocked cautiously on the french window.

She came out of the shadows and looked at me curiously.

'Hello,' she said.

'I wonder if you could help me. I'm looking for Henry and Karen ... Karen!'

'Michael Jackson!'

We embraced, then held each other at arm's length.

'You've gone grey!' Karen said.

'I didn't recognise you!'

'I suppose I've got a few grey hairs, too, if the truth be known. And put on a bit of weight. But you haven't changed. I would have recognised that voice anywhere!'

'It's good to see you,' I said.

'It's good to see you, too.'

We sat out on the deck. I told Karen how overwhelmed I'd been coming down from the Rangitikei country, watching the clouds moving over the hills as over the callused palm of an upturned hand. I did not mention my visit during the winter.

'Nine years is nine years,' Karen said.

'It isn't the time I've been away,' I said. 'It's how quickly and completely I feel at home here.'

'I felt the same when we first arrived,' Karen said. 'I've never felt cut off from the world here, for all the isolation.'

'When you were in Palmerston North you said you didn't want to move.'

'Well, it was hard. I had second thoughts about taking the kids out of school, separating them from their friends. If Henry hadn't been so desperate I would never have done it. "If things don't work out, we can always crawl back to Palmerston and pick up where we left off," he said. "We're not burning our bridges." But of course we were.'

'In the beginning the silence at night used to scare me. I wouldn't step outside the caravan unless there was some light. But as soon as I got to know the place, all that changed. I walked everywhere. The ridge from Takapari to Maharahara. The headwaters of the river. I even walked down to Pohangina! I didn't care if I got lost or didn't get back before dark. I felt in my element everywhere, not just here in the house. And I never got bored. In Palmerston, the truth is I felt housebound and bored half the time.'

The dogs came snuffling and scampering up the stone steps with Henry close behind.

He had grown a black beard. His hair was matted and filthy. In one hand he held a sawn-off shotgun, in the other a blood-streaked haunch of wild pork. He set the meat down on the deck, wiped his hand on his shorts, and we shook hands. We found it awkward to look each other in the eye. Henry began to unstrap the sheath of his bone-handled hunting knife which was laced around his thigh. His legs were cut and smeared with blood and dirt.

'Let me just take care of the dogs,' he said.

Pickle, Flo and Maxwell were bull terriers. They'd been gored by a big boar which Henry had run to earth but then lost track of.

Maxwell had suffered the worst mauling. Henry called him over to a patch of paspalum grass beside the deck. He gently pushed the dog onto its side, lanced its ear with his knife, and injected penicillin into the wound. The dog did not even whimper.

'Doesn't he feel anything?' I asked.

'Not these buggers,' Henry said. 'They don't feel pain.'

Karen announced that Kate was doing some tie-dying in the studio, and promptly disappeared into the manuka with a bolt of muslin which had been propped against the deck rail.

Henry hung his haunch of pork from a verandah post and told me how easy they had it there: vegetables from the garden, fruit and olives from the orchard, pheasant, rabbit, quail, venison and wild pork.

I admitted it seemed like a good life.

'You still drink?' Henry asked.

He fetched a jug of feijoa wine from inside the house, and we drank and talked about old times.

Henry had had a panel-beating business in Palmerston North. We used to play snooker and pool together – Henry, his partner Mac and I. But then Mac rolled his Land Rover and was killed. It was never the same again. One afternoon a few weeks after Mac's funeral, Henry and I were drinking in the Café de Paris. Henry would tell me later that he remembered going for a piss, remembered returning to the bar, the smoke and shouting, the press of bodies. Remembered rejoining me at the bar. But then he was standing there, rooted to the spot, in a kind of stupor. It wasn't that he'd drunk too much, he said. But he was overcome by an unnerving sensation of being utterly remote from everything that was going on around him, that he was seeing everything clearly but was himself unseen. It lasted only a few seconds. The froth slipped slowly down the inside of a drained glass. The bent minute-hand of the wall clock quavered. Two men mouthed incoherent curses into each other's faces. But when the moment passed Henry was saying to himself, 'Hell, is this the rest of my life?'

'So what brings you back?' Henry asked.

I told Henry that I'd been in Auckland for my father's funeral. And I told him something of the book I was researching on the life and times of Joe Pawelka. There were some leads I wanted to follow up in the Manawatu, so I had come back.

'He could have hidden out here and never been found,' Henry said.

He drained the jug and bade me follow him up onto the hill behind the house, clear of the scrub.

He lit a joint, and we passed it to and fro.

The land was glowing in the last light. In their kennels, the exhausted dogs stirred at their chains.

I wanted to share with Henry some of the things that had been going through my mind as I drove south. I wanted to talk about how New Zealand had changed since the '60s.

For as long as I can remember I had felt driven to broaden my horizons. To break out of the parochial world in which I was raised. Protesting New Zealand's complicity in the Vietnam War or sporting contacts with South Africa were definitive moments for my generation, focusing our awareness of the deep, undeniable links between local and global worlds. Then gradually the old insular, nationalistic, rural New Zealand world against which we had railed began to yield to the urbane, intellectually unabashed and internationally conscious world in which we felt more at home. Some of us who had gone abroad thought of returning. And many who had stayed and outgrown the stultifying, repressive influence of the old order turned to reflecting on their history and whakapapa with a new sense of engagement and acceptance. It was as though we were now distant enough from our past to regard it without fear. No longer embarrassed by our backgrounds or in thrall to our innocence, we could move from passing judgement on others to understanding ourselves.

When I told Henry I was thinking of coming back, he said: 'What does it matter where you are? If you put down roots, you end up going to seed.'

'How about you?'

He laughed. 'I'm just going to pot!'

Henry was writing a book. *Pig Hunter's Diary*, he was going to call it.

A couple of years ago he had shot a 140-pound boar. It took him four hours to drag it home through the bush. By the time he finished butchering it, darkness had fallen. He filled the outside bathtub with hot water. A full moon was rising over Takapari. He poured himself a gin and tonic and rolled a joint. Then he climbed into the bath and lay there, sipping his drink, blowing the joint, looking up through the manuka at the stars. 'That's when I got to thinking I should start a diary,' Henry said. 'A pig hunter's diary. Some kind of record of my life here.'

We sat around a trestle table. Candles flickered in jam jars among plates of wild pork and watercress. The doors of the room were flung open to the cicada-shrilling night. I was sitting beside Kate, the last of Henry and Karen's kids still living at home. As she passed me bowls of sweet potatoes, carrots and beetroot, she said I looked as though I needed the nourishment.

'I like your frankness,' I said.

'You're welcome,' she said.

Henry said he was thinking of installing a small electrical turbine. He was sure there would be sufficient fall of water from the stream to drive it. They'd be able to generate enough electricity for some lights and a stereo.

'Oh, God,' Kate muttered. 'He'll be able to play his Grateful Dead records again!'

It delighted me that Kate was as irreverent at fourteen as she had been at five.

'What's your favourite group?' I asked.

'Crowded House,' she said.

After dinner, Karen began clearing the table, asking who wanted coffee and who wanted tea.

I turned to Kate. 'What now?'

'I suppose Mum will want to play her clarinet.'

'Do you play an instrument?'

'Dad tried to teach me the guitar, but what I'd really like is a drum kit.'

'You should ask Michael about the book he's working on,' Henry said.

'Are you writing a book?' Kate asked.

'Have you heard of Butch Cassidy and the Sundance Kid?' I asked.

'No.'

'Butch Cassidy was a notorious American outlaw. I'm working on a book about a man who was a kind of New Zealand Butch Cassidy.' Turning to Henry and Karen, I said: 'You remember how the film about Butch Cassidy and the Sundance Kid ends with a siege and shoot-out in Bolivia in which the outlaws are killed?'

Henry and Karen remembered the film sequence.

'Well, it's true they left the United States and went to South America. But the story that they died in Bolivia was never proven. In all probability, Butch Cassidy returned to the States and began a new life under an assumed name. He visited his family in Utah, kept up a correspondence with an old flame, remarried, began a small manufacturing company, and even wrote an account of his life as an outlaw.'

'What about Joe Pawelka?' Henry asked. 'What happened to him?'

'That's what I'm hoping to find out.'

CZ&O

13

Beyond the Call of Duty

When I began my second stint of research on Joe Pawelka, my most pressing concern was to trace members of his family. So far I had wound up in archives and cemeteries. Like the winter day I walked over a windswept hill near Kimbolton where lichen-covered graves huddled among laurels, box and yew. There was a cold wind blowing across the Oroua valley, threatening rain, and I did not stay long. And I found no Pawelkas; only a lopsided white wooden cross with the name Agnes Elizabeth Hansen painted on a strip of tin. Joe Pawelka's oldest sister had died only nine years ago.

In Wellington, Richard Hill, the official police historian, had urged me to get in touch with Ray Carter. Ray was a retired senior constable; he'd interviewed members of the Pawelka family when researching his history of the Palmerston North police district and he might give me some leads. So I had written to Ray Carter, mentioning my grandfather and my long-standing interest in Joe Pawelka, and in reply Ray invited me to visit him when I was next in Palmerston North.

Following Joe Pawelka's trail into the land of the living made me unsure of my ground. As I drove in from the Pohangina, the air was heavy with the smells of lupin, clover and river water. Everywhere I sensed the pencilled shadows, the held breath, of poplars.

Ray's house was white stucco, with a neat lawn and concrete driveway. The front door was a pane of frosted glass, a tulle curtain inside. I pressed the doorbell anxiously.

Ray seemed not at all suspicious. He led me into the sitting room and invited me to sit down. A copy of the *Manawatu Evening Standard* lay open on the coffee table. The front page story was about a kidnapping at gunpoint and high-speed car chase through the Manawatu. Ray was surprised I hadn't heard about it. There was so much violent crime these days, he said. Things were going from bad to worse. In his entire police career he had carried a firearm only once. But now ....

'It was the same in my grandfather's day,' I said. 'He carried a truncheon. He said that if you carried a gun you had to be ready to use it, and he didn't want to risk that.'

'Nowadays the armed offenders' squad is out all the time,' Ray said.

We chatted for a while about the stresses of police work. Then Ray took a slip of paper from a conjurer's table and passed it to me.

It gave details of my grandfather's police service, including his six years between 1908 and 1915 stationed in Levin. Fred Longbottom. No.: 1267. Born: England 21 October 1877. Sworn: 26 June 1906. Retired on pension: 13 December 1943.

Ray explained that a new police station had just been opened in Levin. He had assembled a large collection of old photographs for the occasion, but hadn't been able to lay his hands on a photo of my grandfather. Perhaps I had one I could send him?

'I suppose he took a lot of flak because of his name,' Ray said.

'Being called Longbottom can't have been any more bothersome than being called Michael Jackson,' I said. I told Ray that I envied my grandfather's thick skin. When friends urged him to change his name by deed poll to Long, he wouldn't hear of it.

'In the force they called him Longy,' Ray said.

As we reminisced, I began to relax. I realised how fortuitous it was that my grandfather had been a cop. It made it easier for me to broach the subject of Joe Pawelka.

When Ray offered to make coffee or tea, I said I'd like a cup of tea, and followed him into the kitchen where he put on the kettle and emptied some biscuits out of a packet. When I asked Ray about the conjuring table in the other room, he explained that he was secretary of the local magic club.

I told Ray that my grandfather had been a constable in Halifax at the time Harry Houdini made his famous tour of England. He'd been in Bradford in 1901 when Houdini escaped from a locked cell in the police station. My grandfather admired Houdini and used to tell me stories about his various stunts and athletic feats.

'An interesting coincidence,' I said, 'was that Houdini was on tour in Australia in March and April 1910, performing his escapes from handcuffs and straitjackets at the same time Joe Pawelka broke out of prison and did his vanishing act.'

Ray confessed that he had not dug very deeply into the Pawelka story. After all, it had been just one item among many that he'd had to research for *Beyond the Call of Duty*, his history of the Palmerston North police district. But he had gone up to Kimbolton in July 1985 and interviewed Joe Pawelka's sister.

'I think Agnes got fed up with reporters over the years,' Ray said. 'She'd been so pestered by people wanting to know what happened to her brother that she clammed up.'

Talking to Agnes, Ray had been careful not to pry. He neither referred to her brother's crimes nor to his escape from prison. He'd been forewarned that he'd be shown the door if he did. But the conversation went well, and Ray felt that Agnes trusted him. When her son Jack came to take her to a doctor's appointment in Feilding, Agnes invited Ray to come back some time and talk with her again.

But Ray never did go back. A few weeks later, his wife died of cancer. And Agnes died the same month, aged 96. Ray remembered the exact date because it fell so soon after his wife's death.

'It was the same with my interview with Jack Hansen,' Ray said. 'I began to interview him, but never followed it up.'

But he did learn something that might interest me. Sometime during World War I, Joe's parents received a photo of a group of soldiers clipped from a newspaper. There were about thirty soldiers in the photograph. They were in a desert somewhere. Around one of the soldiers in the back row a circle had been drawn. The family were unable to decipher the postmark on the envelope, and there was no letter to indicate who had sent the photo or why.

I asked Ray if he minded my making some notes.

He didn't mind; he was only sorry he couldn't help me more. He'd felt the same when Joe Pawelka's granddaughter came to see him, asking if he could tell her something about her grandfather.

I was astounded. 'His granddaughter?' I said.

Ray related how early in 1984 he was visited by a woman who had travelled up from Wellington with her son. She told Ray that only two weeks before she had learned of the identity of her grandfather. Her name was Anne Harris. Her mother's maiden name was Iris Wilson.

Up to that moment, Ray had taken only a passing interest in Joe Pawelka. Now he was stunned to discover not only the existence of Joe's granddaughter but the fact that an old friend with whom he'd travelled to England and France thirty years ago for a scout jamboree, was Anne's ex-husband.

After I had copied Anne's address and telephone number into my notebook, our talk drifted away from Joe Pawelka. Ray pointed out photos of his wife on the china cabinet and mantlepiece. Then he showed me a photo of himself in dress uniform, with the Governor-General pinning a medal to his chest. It was the Queen's Medal, he explained. He received it the year he retired. It was an odd thing. For years he and his wife used to scan the birthday honours list and joke about his name not being included. Then one day he picked up the paper and was incredulous to see his name on the list. If only she had been alive to share it with him, to remember how they joked for all those years about his name being omitted.

I said it was strange that I had lived in Palmerston North for almost ten years yet our paths had never crossed.

Ray said he had policed the Massey campus during the '70s, but didn't remember meeting me.

'I must have been keeping out of trouble,' I said.

As Ray rambled on with anecdotes about his police days, I kept thinking of the ways in which the stories we tell reshape the experiences we have had and often eclipse our memory of an actual event. Perhaps this explains why people who commit what they consider a justified crime protest their innocence with such conviction. The story of what occurred is gradually supplanted by the story told in mitigation.

When I asked Ray about this kind of misprision, he said he was all too familiar with it. 'It's very typical of sex offenders,' he said. 'They often imagine that their victim was a willing party to the act and even derived pleasure from it.'

Ray described how some years ago, when he was relieving at Woodville, a man came into the police station and asked to see Constable X, who was normally in charge there. 'He's away for a month,' Ray told him. The man asked Ray if he could speak to him in private. When they were alone, the man confessed to sex offences he'd committed in 1948. He couldn't live with the memory of what he'd done. He had to own up. Ray wrote down the names of the two girls who had been molested. He told the man he would look into the matter. The police traced one of the girls. She was now a married woman with three children. She did not want to talk about what had happened all those years ago. She'd tried to forget. There was no question of taking action. Of prosecuting. It was past, and she wanted to bury it in the past.

'Do you think Joe Pawelka's family also wanted to forget the past?'

'Forget, perhaps. But whether they ever forgave him is another matter. You should talk to Jack Hansen about that.'

Jack Hansen, I now learned, was Joe Pawelka's nephew.

ॐ

14

Talking to Jack Hansen

In 1890 Cornelis J. Hansen owned a drapery shop on the Palmerston Square. A canny businessman, he travelled the Manawatu in a horse-drawn dray, selling haberdashery and bartering needles, thread, ribbons and fabric for a side of lamb or other farm produce.

With its bracing air and invigorating climate, Kimbolton was the one place where he found respite from his asthma. He moved there in 1891 and established premises in the main street. A couple of years later, his son William took over the business and opened a general store. The Pawelkas were among his first customers.

When I went up to Kimbolton to meet Jack Hansen, the store looked much the same as it did in photos taken a hundred years ago: clapboard exterior, verandah roofed with corrugated iron, seven verandah posts with wrought iron capitals ... though *HANSEN'S STORE* on the fascia had been temporarily painted out.

Jack Hansen was the third generation Hansen to have run the store. He was born there, lived there all his life, and never married.

The floor of the shop was covered with worn, brown body carpet. I took in the ubiquitous Tip Top ice cream signs, racks of chocolate

Hansen's store, Kimbolton, May 1995 (the lettering on the facade has since been repainted: C.J. Hansen and Sons, General Store).

bars and potato chips, shelves of tinned food and cornflakes. In the corner was the usual collection of Sylvester Stallone and Chuck Norris videos.

I explained to the man behind the counter that I was looking for Jack Hansen. Jack had a flat out the back, I was told. If I walked through the shop I'd see his door. 'Just knock and go on in. He's always there.'

Jack was sitting in a fireside chair. He levered himself up and stood shakily for a moment as I introduced myself. I mentioned Ray Carter, and explained that I had come from the United States to do some research on Joe.

We shook hands, and Jack gestured for me to sit down.

'I hope the weather stays good,' he said. 'You never know what it's going to do at this time of year.'

To broach the subject of Joe Pawelka I referred to the stories my grandfather told me when I was a boy and my grandfather's opinion that Joe had got a raw deal. I also told Jack that I had lived in the

Manawatu for nine years, and had always wanted to know what happened to Joe and where he ended up.

Jack's wry look unsettled me. I had a strong sense that I was broaching matters which were none of my business. I was presuming too much, and would be told nothing.

'Well, he must have been a superman to have committed all those crimes,' Jack said drily. And waited.

I mentioned the photo that Ray had described to me.

Jack remembered the photo. He had no idea what had become of it. It was actually a photo Joe's mother clipped from a newspaper – of a group of American or Canadian soldiers in France. Louisa was convinced that one of the soldiers in the photo was Joe. 'She was absolutely sure it was he. I – I don't know. I suppose it could've looked like somebody ... but then, would a mother know her own child?'

'Perhaps it was wishful thinking. Something for her to hang on to ....'

'Yeah. I think that's one of the reasons. She'd made up her mind it was him. That would give her some peace of mind. He promised to write. But he never did. I'll never forgive him for that. Because he broke his promise to his mother.'

I asked if Joe's family ever spoke of him.

'Seldom, if ever,' Jack said. It was only when he was in his twenties and asked outright that he was told anything. The family kept its own counsel. Partly it was fear of prosecution for having aided and abetted the fugitive. Partly it was shame – because of the ill-repute Joe brought upon them. 'It was hard,' Jack said. 'It was always hard for the mother.'

'You say the family gave him shelter?'

Jack reminded me that he was born in 1913, a couple of years after Joe's final gaol break, so much of his knowledge was hearsay. 'The family never said much. But everyone felt sorry for him. He'd been so unfairly treated.' Jack was sure that a warder or policeman must have had a hand in helping Joe escape from the Terrace Gaol in Wellington. Leaving a door open. Leaving the way clear.

'My grandfather thought so too,' I said. 'But from what I've read it was his prison cohorts who helped him get away. They saw him as a victim of injustice, even more so than themselves. A kind of hero.'

'People helped him up here, too,' Jack said.

Jack gave me the impression that the entire Kimbolton community closed ranks to keep Joe hidden during the six months between the spring of 1911 and the summer of 1912. Jack's father, who was married to Joe's sister Agnes, was actively involved. 'Dad had a finger in the pie,' Jack said, 'if he wasn't the whole pie.'

Opposite Lowe's Boarding House on the corner of Grammar Street and Kimbolton Road there used to be a general store and row of outbuildings that belonged to Jack and Hilton Fowler. The last building in the row was a grainstore. It was here that Willie Hansen hid his brother-in-law, Joe Pawelka. Years later, the Kiwitea County Council bought the buildings and converted the old grainstore into a garage. When the floorboards of the grainstore were torn up in preparation for pouring a concrete slab, some musty old prison clothes were discovered. Supposing them to have belonged to Joe Pawelka, the Council presented them to Willie Hansen as a souvenir.

'Do you think your father was sympathetic to Joe, or was he simply being loyal to your mother's family in helping him out?'

'I think possibly because Joe was his brother-in-law, and he wanted him out of the way ....' Jack chuckled, '... out of his ....'

Jack's laughter left the sentence hanging.

'Hair?' I wanted to say, but instead I asked: 'Did your father ever tell you what happened to Joe? Did Joe's fate concern him?'

'I don't think it worried him.'

'He didn't ever try to find out whether ....'

'No. No,' Jack said slowly, but with finality. 'I don't think so.'

'Just getting him out of the district was enough? He'd done his job?' I said.

'He'd done his job, yeah.'

'Yet everyone in Kimbolton knew what your father was up to?'

'Everyone knew. Joe's mum cooked meals for him. Willie conveyed them over the road to Joe. And Joe used to help his father down at the forest reserve. I think the local vicar walked in on them one day. But he never spilled the beans. Even the local constable turned a blind eye.'

It was hard to know how accurate this observation was. At the time of Joe's escape, the police assumed he would try to see Lizzie again. Believing they would 'get this man through his wife', they kept a close watch on the Wilson house in Ashhurst. It was also thought likely that Joe would return home.

On 11 October 1911, six weeks after Joe's escape, Sergeant Bowden went up to Kimbolton from Feilding to interview Willie Hansen. In his report, written the same day, Bowden noted: 'Mr Hansen says personally he has never seen Pawelka since he came out of the Palmerston North hospital that was before his trouble commenced.' Willie Hansen assured Bowden that he 'did not assist or succour Pawelka at any time, and he was quite sure his wife did not, as she had none of his money to do it with.'

Hansen went on to say that if Joe was still in the country 'his friends are keeping him safe, but if he had got out of the country and could keep away it will be a good job' – implying that Joe was so attached to his wife and child that he would go to any lengths to see them. When Bowden asked Hansen if he thought that Pawelka had left New Zealand, Hansen replied, 'Oh, God knows where he is, but one thing is certain, sooner or later he will see his wife and child if they remain at Ashhurst.'

At the end of the interview, Hansen and Bowden shook hands.

'Well, Sergeant,' said Hansen, 'Joe is a miracle to get away as he did. God knows where he has got to.'

Bowden may have taken Willie Hansen's remarks with a grain of salt. Two weeks after talking to Hansen, he ordered Constable Fitzgibbon at Kimbolton to 'carefully approach Mr Hansen and ascertain if possible if he or any of the family has heard of the whereabouts of the escaped prisoner.'

Fitzgibbon spoke to Hansen two days after Bowden interviewed him, and filed his report on 28 October 1911.

Apparently, Willie Hansen volunteered the remark that he had given Bowden 'the straight lip'. Sooner or later, Pawelka was bound to visit Ashhurst. Fitzgibbon asked if this view was founded on facts.

> Hansen replied well to be candid with you Yes. Hansen further stated I have heard through his relatives that he was making for Ashhurst and I expected he would turn up there long before now, but apparently he has been headed off or some of his friends might have warned him that he was watched there. I have not seen Joe since he got out, and I don't know his whereabouts, But I know for a fact he has not left the country. I don't know what the police think of Joe but it is my opinion the man is mad in fact he is a lunatic he gets into mad fits at times, I don't know if it is through bad temper or not, but when he is in one of his mad fits he is dangerous, from what I have heard from Joe's relatives and it is also my opinion that Joe will visit Ashurst *[sic]* to see his Child and if he turns up there in one of his mad fits I am afraid he would murder his wife, that is of course providing she didn't receive him with open arms, but if she did things might be different, but as far as I am aware I don't think his wife has any time for him. Joe might

change his mind and try to leave the Country, but this in my opinion is not a very easy matter to do. He must get impatient in time, and if the Police play a waiting game they are sure to catch him.

Fitzgibbon concluded his report: 'I have carefully questioned Hansen but could obtain no further information from him. It is my opinion Hansen is not assisting the prisoner, but I do beleive [sic] he could give information as to prisoner's whereabouts, but this he would not disclose.'

It's difficult to establish whether or not Fitzgibbon was part of a local conspiracy to shelter the fugitive. At the time he wrote his report he had been stationed in Kimbolton only fifteen months, though he would remain there for a further nine years. Whether loyalty to the community took precedence over loyalty to his office, one cannot judge. In Moabite, my grandfather sometimes bent the rules or turned a blind eye on minor infractions of the law such as after-hours drinking, but helping an escaped prisoner evade justice was another matter. The story of Fitzgibbon's involvement is probably an artefact of our egalitarian ethos.

Indeed, it recalls a story Richard Hill tells about an Otira policeman whose best mate was allegedly Joe Pawelka. Given the absence of evidence that the policeman in question had any criminal mates, one may suppose that the anecdote is born of a collective desire to erase the differences between authority figures and underlings. Like the notion that prison officers rather than fellow prisoners helped Pawelka escape from the Terrace Gaol.

Then there was the vexing matter of Willie Hansen's vilification of his brother-in-law. Informing the police that Joe was most likely to head for Ashhurst could have been a clever ruse. Are we to suppose that calling Joe a lunatic was also a device to throw Fitzgibbon off the scent? Or was there more ambivalence in Joe Pawelka's home town than legend would care to admit? I found it difficult to dismiss from my mind the derogatory way Willie Hansen had spoken about his brother-in-law when interviewed by a newspaper man at the height of the manhunt, particularly his assertion that Pawelka would 'get no sympathy from his people'.

I asked Jack if there had been bad blood between the Hansens and the Pawelkas. After all, Millar and Giorgi's drapery shop, which Joe allegedly burgled and burned to the ground on 5 April 1910, was, according to newspaper reports at the time, owned by Cornelis J. Hansen. Did Joe have a grudge against Hansen? If so, did this grudge have anything to do with the fact that Joe's sister, Agnes, had married a Hansen two years before?

Jack said my account was 'not quite correct'. C.J. Hansen's shop was next door to Millar and Giorgi's. Joe wouldn't have set fire to the draper's because his father-in-law's shop would have gone up in flames as well. 'Anyway, Joe wouldn't have held a grudge against my father, because really my father protected Joe very much.'

In fact, Millar and Giorgi's *was* leased from C.J. Hansen. Perhaps Pawelka hadn't known this, or hadn't cared. But I didn't want to press the matter. Not that I despaired at resolving it. It was more a question of discretion and tact. And after all, my real interest was in gleaning information about Joe's ultimate fate.

I asked Jack if he had read Des Swain's book, *Pawelka*.

'I've got a copy, yes.'

'Was Des Swain correct in saying that Joe travelled to Auckland by overnight train and boarded a ship for Vancouver?'

Jack affirmed that this was true.

'Why Canada?'

'No idea.'

Jack described how his father got a Masonic brother and close friend, a local farmer called Sam Hall, to buy the train and boat tickets. 'They hatched the plan out on his farm.' The Pawelkas,

Hansens and Willie Hansen's friend scraped up the money for the fare. It was decided that a young man called Ted Lawrence, who worked on the farm, would accompany Joe to Auckland. 'They knew Lawrence could be trusted. That's how he came into the picture.'

'Was Ted Lawrence a mate of Joe's?'

'No, no. Didn't know him. No, he just worked for this great friend of Dad's.'

'Are there Lawrences still in the district?'

'No. No. Ted'd be dead many years, and I think his son .... I think he's dead, too, now.'

'Anyone I could contact?'

'No. At any rate, Lawrence wouldn't have dared mention it in case he was ....'

'Accessory after the fact.'

'Yeah. So his family wouldn't have known what their father got up to.'

'So Ted took Joe up to Mangaweka?'

'No, Joe's father took him to Mangaweka, hidden under sacks in a dray.'

'Then where did Ted board the train?'

'At Mangaweka, I think. I think they met at Mangaweka.'

February. Mid-summer. The overnight train pulled into Mangaweka in the evening. So it would have been daylight. It must have been a nerve-racking moment.

Next day in Auckland, Ted and Joe had only a short walk from the railway station to the new Queen Street Wharf where Joe was to board a ship bound for Canada.

Having got Joe onto the boat, Ted went ashore. He returned to say goodbye not long before the boat sailed, but couldn't find Joe anywhere. So there was no certainty that Joe actually sailed.

I wanted to press Jack further on this, but hesitated. I knew that

Des Swain had interviewed Helen, and had been unable to take Joe's story beyond the point I had reached with Jack. I had to assume that Agnes would have shared what she knew with her son. And I did not think Jack was prevaricating.

I glanced around the room. On either side of the fireplace were shelves of Agnes's old books. Frank Slaughter, Frances Parkinson Keyes, Frank L. Packard, A.J. Cronin. The same books my grandfather used to read. On the mantlepiece, a clock, vases of artificial flowers and family photos, including one of Jack's mother Agnes in her 94th year.

'You know, it's a pity you didn't get started on your research a bit sooner,' Jack said, 'when my mother was alive. And my Aunt Helen. She died only last July. She might have been able to help you, too.'

I felt I had come to the end of the road.

'There's not a lot I can tell you,' Jack went on. 'Not a lot that's known. Like I said, it's mostly hearsay.'

'It must be difficult, living with so many things unresolved,' I said. 'So much unfinished business.' I didn't mean the rifts that might exist in the town. I meant the impossibility of ever knowing for certain what became of Joe after Ted Lawrence last saw him in Auckland.

Jack didn't seem to hear. He wanted to know what I planned to do with my research. What use I was going to make of it.

I said I was thinking of writing a book.

'A lot of nonsense has been written,' Jack said, and promptly asked if I'd seen the film about Pawelka that had been shown on TV a few years ago. 'Rubbish!' he exclaimed. 'It was all about the shooting of McGuire. All the scandal. Everything made so melodramatic.'

Jack recalled a conversation with the producer/director, Allan Lindsay. Lindsay had requested an interview, and Jack agreed to a meeting in Feilding.

'I didn't want Mum to be a part of it,' Jack said. So while he met the film-maker in the Catholic presbytery, Agnes went into the church and spent the time on her knees in prayer.

By the end of the interview, Jack felt very uneasy.

'You got any family?' he asked the film-maker.

'Yes.'

'Let's hope it doesn't happen to them.'

Jack meant the shame and exposure.

For as long as his mother lived he 'vetted' the daily paper before she saw it, clipping out items that might rub salt into her wounds. He still had the clippings in an envelope somewhere.

'She kept her hurt and her thoughts to herself,' Jack said. 'But people kept wanting to drag it all out into the open again.'

When the Centennial Exhibition opened in Wellington in 1940 it included a 'Chamber of Horrors' with a tableau showing Joe Pawelka's recapture in the Ashhurst cow byre. There were empty beer bottles on the hay bales, and Pawelka had pistols drawn.

'It made me sick,' Jack said. 'I hadn't been bothered much up 'til then, but I felt hurt at what I saw.'

'Shame?'

'It was the shock that upset me. Not shame. It was never spoken of in the house, you see. I was shocked and upset seeing what had been kept in the dark now so exposed, so public.'

I said that these were the things I found least compelling. It was the way Joe Pawelka's life touched our lives even now that intrigued me.

Jack said nothing and I judged it was time to go. We stood up together and shook hands. I told Jack I was grateful to him for talking to me. 'It can't be easy, dealing with some stranger who turns up out of the blue, asking a lot of vexing questions.'

Jack assured me that he had enjoyed our conversation. He was only sorry he could not help me more.

The sunlight was blinding as I crossed the road to the Commercial Hotel where there were some photos I wanted to see.

The bar was deserted but the proprietor came out from a back room and asked if there was anything he could get me. I said I wanted to see some of the old photos in the front bar. Could I walk through?

There was one photo, considerably enlarged, of Lowe's Family and Commercial Hotel in 1901 or 1902. Standing in front of the hotel were the proprietor and his wife, three maids in pinafores (possibly the proprietor's daughters), and a few locals. There were also two gigs and Sam Daw's mail coach from Feilding.

The proprietor watched me from the bar as I scrutinised the photo.

'That young man standing in the road, that's Joe Pawelka,' he said.

I looked hard. Pawelka would have been thirteen or fourteen at the time.

'He was a hard case,' the proprieter said, and began regaling me with stories about how Joe lived in barns and sheds, and locals smuggled food and clothing to him. According to some reports, he was hidden for a while in the big warehouse behind Hansen's shop, which was always kept locked. At one time he was hidden under the floorboards of the shed which used to stand on the corner opposite the hotel. Often he was brought into the hotel at night for a hot bath and a square meal. No one gave him away, although one day his eight-year old sister, Helen, came home from school at lunchtime accompanied by a friend, to fetch a book she had forgotten, and found him sitting in the kitchen ....

Driving back to the Pohangina Valley that afternoon, I kept thinking of the effect Joe's disappearance must have had on his family. For the police and the newspapers, his disappearance was a mystery to be solved, a case to be closed. For the family, it was a matter of surviving a loss whose true character might never be known. Of trying to find the fugitive shape of an ending for Joe's story in the story of their own lives. I was reminded of things I had read about Butch Cassidy who, like Joe Pawelka, grew up in a poor rural family, was a first-born son, got into crime, and became the focus of popular sympathy and the stuff of legend. What did *his* family think and feel during the years Butch was in South America, before he came back to the States to begin a new life under an assumed name?

When in her nineties, Lula Parker-Betenson related the story of her brother, Robert Parker (Butch Cassidy) to a ghost writer, she struggled to explain why he had become an outlaw. 'Did he see too few roses and too many thorns?' she asked. 'Too few rainbows and too many dark clouds?' She felt her brother had been 'a victim of his early choices'. 'He was trapped by his reputation; he could not escape it.' But for Lula, the real tragedy was not his, but his family's. 'He didn't realise that when he went to prison, a whole family was sentenced with him, especially Mother and Dad. Even though he escaped retribution so many times by evading the law, we felt the full impact of his crimes. No amount of rationalising that he was Robin Hood – taking from the rich and giving to the poor – could relieve our parents of the terrible load they carried every day of their lives because of him .... Mother's heart was broken over this wayward son. Her prayers remained unanswered. Even though we were a fun-loving lot, always there was the undercurrent of shame and humiliation .... Mother was 58 when she died, and I have always felt she literally died of a broken heart.'

I was also reminded of Robyn Jensen's story, which had recently been reviewed in an Auckland paper.

Robyn Jensen's daughter Kirsa disappeared in the spring of 1983 when she was fourteen. Kirsa was probably murdered. The prime suspect killed himself in 1992. Kirsa's body was never found. For months, then years, Robyn Jensen had to endure not knowing what had happened to her daughter. 'We were in a vacuum,' she said. 'Our grief was stationary. We were not able to move to the next step because there was no next step.' One of the worst things for Robyn Jensen was the way the media appropriated the tragedy. Writing a book, in which she wrested back control of Kirsa's story, brought a kind of freedom, helping her reclaim what had been taken from her. But it provided no real ending. 'There is no conclusion, no resolution,' she said, 'until Kirsa is returned to me.'

Late that afternoon Henry, Karen, Kate and I went down to the river with a hamper of cold meats, home-baked bread, black olives and a spinach salad.

As Karen shared out the food and Henry uncorked a bottle of his feijoa wine, I spoke of my conversation with Jack Hansen and of the fear in which the Pawelka family lived after aiding and abetting Joe's escape from New Zealand. 'But the worst of it must have been the distress of never knowing for certain what had happened to him, the impossibility of ever drawing the story of his life to a close.'

'Why not write your own ending?' Henry suggested. 'Isn't that what writers are licensed to do?'

'I wouldn't do that,' I said. 'The truth might not always be stranger than fiction, but it's usually a lot more compelling.'

'What you were saying reminds me of my uncle,' Karen said. 'He's now in his late seventies. He was adopted when he was a baby. His parents kept the truth from him until he was grown up, and then it was too late for him to trace his birth parents. Now it obsesses him. He says his life has been a travesty. The only thing that matters to him now is to know who his mother and father really were. To know their names. How they came to have him. Why they gave him away.'

I said: 'It's like those times when someone calls you and you're not at home, but instead of leaving a message on your answering machine the caller leaves nothing but a long silence.'

'Or when the phone rings,' Karen said, 'and you don't get to it in time, and you're left wondering who on earth it was who called.'

Henry read the sky. He pointed out the hogsbacks and mare's tails over the Ruahines, and said we were in for a change.

'I think I'll head south tomorrow,' I said.

'Must you go so soon?' Karen asked.

'There's someone I have to see in Wellington,' I said.

That night it rained. I lay awake listening to the rain's soft flow and patter on the iron roof.

> ... *one writes to close an account. To make good a loss. Creating ghost dialogues in one's own mind in order to reach an understanding that was never quite reached in life. One writes to fill a gap that life has left in one's soul. In the artifice of closure is the hope of renewal. Which is why storytelling is akin to the healing arts. A way of making things whole.*

In the darkness, Henry's pig dogs yelped at their chains.

ೞ&ಐ

15

Passing Strange

Driving south through the rain-rinsed landscape, macrocarpas massed against the morning as though they had soaked up the night and were hoarding it. Was my search for Joe Pawelka 'a wild goose chase', to use one of my father's favourite phrases? An attempt to recapture my own past?

At the turn off to the Ohariu Valley Road near Johnsonville, the road signs were silhouetted riders. Anne Harris's house was tucked into an armpit of the hill, a corner of the switchback road. There were ceramic pots and urns in the yard. Blue agapanthus, sweetpeas and daisies.

Anne came out to greet me. Had I had any trouble following her directions? She invited me into a sunlit living room. Beyond the north-facing windows, the hills were cusped like molars.

'I'm just making a pot of tea,' Anne said. 'Or would you prefer coffee?'

There was a tape recorder on the coffee table, and a shallow bowl filled with sprigs of rosemary and slices of lemon.

'To help the memory,' Anne said. 'I'm so interested in finding out everything I can, but half the time I don't make a proper record of what I do find out, so today I'm prepared.'

It took me aback that Anne should think I might enlighten *her*. But I was glad there'd be a record of our conversation. I wouldn't have to take notes. We'd be free to talk.

After pouring the tea, Anne switched on the tape recorder, and I began telling her how I had become interested in her grandfather through my own grandfather's stories.

Anne said she had learned of the identity of her grandfather only ten years ago. Joe's younger sister, Florence Helen Pawelka, had married Duncan Bryce. It had been their son, John Bryce, who had contacted her in early 1984 when he was doing genealogical research on his own family. This was the first time in her life she'd had any inkling of who her mother's father really was.

'Why do you think your mother kept you in the dark?' I asked.

'She wanted to forget it. It had such a terrible impact on her life. They felt they couldn't talk about it. But it was all so unnecessary, that flagellation.'

'How did you feel when you discovered the truth?'

'I was totally aghast that I'd never been told. And very hurt. Hurt that mother didn't feel I was a suitable person to tell. She told my brother, after all.'

'It must have been hard on your mother. On her mother, too. Always wondering if Joe would turn up again. Never being able to get over the misfortune of her marriage.'

'It was tough. Pretty tough. My grandmother brought my mother up on her own. She reverted to her maiden name. But I guess, had I known the story, I probably would have seen ....' Anne hesitated. 'Lizzie died relatively young. She was born in 1881, and died in 1945 ....'

Anne opened up a scrapbook in which she'd written details of her lineage.

The Wilsons had emigrated from England on the *Edwin Fox* in 1878. They hailed from Rosedale, Yorkshire. Joseph was a farm labourer. His wife, Hannah, had already borne seven children. They settled in Nelson for a while, then moved to Ashhurst. Lizzie was born there in 1881, her mother's last child. Joseph died there in 1900.

Anne said she was struck by a recurrent motif in her family history. Hannah had been sixty-three when her husband died. Her youngest daughter, Hannah Elizabeth, was only thirteen at the time. So little Hannah, or Lizzie as she was called, grew up without a father. More significantly, she was made to fill the emotional void that Joseph's death had left in Hannah's life. This deep bond between mother and daughter may have made it difficult for Hannah to let Lizzie have a life of her own. Even if Joe Pawelka had been a 'suitable boy' in her eyes, he could not but be seen as a threat to her relationship with her last-born.

Hannah Elizabeth Wilson (Granny Wilson), circa 1925.

'How did the motif recur?'

Anne explained that Lizzie was also destined to raise *her* daughter, Iris, alone. So, generation after generation, the shaping influence in the lives of these women was their mothers. The fathers were absent.

I mentioned to Anne the unflattering portrait that had often been drawn of her grandmother. Like Rosina Pawelka, Hannah Wilson is seen as a domineering woman, meddling in her children's lives, trying to control their destinies.

'Old Granny Wilson was a very strong lady,' Anne said. 'She may have felt that her daughter had married beneath her.'

'What of Lizzie?'

Anne felt that it was unfair to blame Lizzie for everything that went wrong in her brief marriage to Joe Pawelka. 'She was a very gentle person. She played the piano. She never struck me as domineering.'

Anne showed me a photo of herself with Lizzie. There is a pine tree, a paddock. Gorse. The old lady is holding something in her hand and smiling as her granddaughter, Anne, reaches up for it. Anne was one-and-a-half when the photo was taken, but has no memory of the occasion.

'Where do you think Joe went wrong?'

'Was it just a bad break?' Anne asked. 'He married a woman six years older than himself. That may have meant more in those days. And he was just a butcher. Didn't have much money. And I can imagine my grandmother, with her mother in the background, probably telling her, "He's not good enough for you ...." '

The sun streamed through the windows. The convoluted landscape was lost in the summer haze.

When Anne discovered that her grandfather was Joe Pawelka, she sought from Helen, Joe's youngest sister, some insight into the kind of person he had been. Though Helen had been only eight when her brother disappeared, she was now Anne's sole link to him, and she didn't want to lose it.

'We had an understanding,' Anne said. If Helen died, it was agreed that she would try to get in touch with Anne from the other side. 'When you go, you must contact me,' Anne told her. 'When I hear you've gone, I'll be waiting by the fireplace.'

I glanced at the fireplace in the shadows of the room.

'Funnily enough, the night after she died, I woke suddenly at two in the morning. I was suddenly wide awake. I got out of bed and came down here, and wandered around, but I couldn't think of anything, so I went back to bed. Next morning I did the same. By this time, I knew she had died. So I sat down here and tried to clear my mind of everything. Then I remembered that the night before I had been searching through some letters, and I'd pulled out one particular envelope and put it on the breakfast table. I hadn't even looked at the name on it. It was the last letter Helen had written to me. I thought to myself, well there are ways ... and I prefer to believe that she was trying, in her way, to communicate with me.'

'It reminds me of Joe's promise to get in touch,' I said.

'Well, maybe he did manage.'

Anne told me how a spiritualist helped her communicate with Joe.

The spirit medium had stood in the middle of the room with a divining-rod. Almost at once, his divining-rod swung toward the south wall. 'Is there anything of your grandfather's in the house?' the spiritualist asked. Anne realised that a pokerwork tray which Joe had made, and which Helen had given her as a memento, was on top of a cabinet in that part of the room.

Anne fetched the tray to show me. There were some flowers and foliage in bas-relief on a pocked square of poker-burned plywood.

'Joe had an artistic side,' Anne said.

With this tray, the diviner had been able to get in touch with 'the other side'. His finding was that Joe had got as far as Hawaii, only to die in an accident there. When Lizzie passed away in 1945, she and Joe were reunited.

'This is my theory,' Anne said. 'It's what I think happened.'

I was struck by the fact that Anne thought Hawaii to have been Joe's last landfall, because she had stopped over in Honolulu herself a few years ago on her way to Canada for a holiday. She'd even checked the Honolulu telephone directory for Pawelkas. In her longing to find out what had happened to her grandfather, had she conflated her journey with his?

To blur the line between what we imagine happened and what actually did occur is perhaps the only way we can live with the past. For when the past is shut out of the present, it becomes alien and menacing. It must be brought in from the darkness continually, to be reconciled with the life we actually live.

So our conversation ended. Anne let me borrow the tape to copy or transcribe. I promised to send it back to her within a few days. I also said that I would get in touch if I came up with anything new. Then I went back to Wellington where I had started my research.

Unfortunately, Anne had used an old answering machine tape and only a few snatches of our conversation were audible. So much for Anne's resolve to 'make a proper record' of whatever she found out.

But I transcribed what I could and jotted down other details of our conversation from memory.

The tape ran on.

It was an old message from Anne's answering machine.

'Jeanette Strange again. We'll get to each other one day. Bye.'

Then silence.

ᛊ

16

Still Life
with Lading Lists

It was 2 in the morning. I could not sleep. My mind was in turmoil, overtaxed by the events of the day. I remembered yellow roadsigns of silhouetted riders, the hills like molars in the haze. The grisly flotsam and jetsam of the police museum still floated on the surface of my mind.

It had been Ray Carter who'd told me about the disguises. Rumour was that when Pawelka escaped from the Lambton Quay lock-up in March 1910 he'd used a disguise. A wig and grease-paint were now on display in the New Zealand Police Museum at the Royal New Zealand Police College in Porirua. So on my way back to Wellington I called there and asked if I could see the forensic collection.

A policewoman at the front desk said the museum wasn't open to the public.

What procedure should I follow, then, to get permission to do research in the museum?

Grudgingly, the policewoman phoned the curator.

'He'll come down and see you,' she said.

While I waited, I studied the enlarged photo of Pawelka's 'wanted' notice on display in the foyer.

The curator was most helpful. He'd heard of the Pawelka disguises. They were supposedly in the old museum at Trentham, though he'd never seen them or spoken to anyone who had. 'In five years here, I've never found them. I don't really think they were ever here.'

But he was prepared to search through some computer indexes and rummage around in the museum storeroom.

I followed him upstairs, where he unlocked the doors to the museum.

I walked into a veritable chamber of horrors. Glass cases filled with meat cleavers, saws, axes, and makeshift murder weapons. A colour photo of a bombed house. Another of a flayed body, its entrails spilling out. The man had been dragged beside a car along a tar-sealed road.

Then a series of macabre black and white photos documenting the notorious floating suitcase murder. A young man, bullied and browbeaten by his father, killed the old man and dismembered the body with a tenon saw. He then stuffed his father's remains into several suitcases, and threw them into the sea from the inter-island ferry. The suitcases did not sink. Here was the thuggish head, squashed, bruised and sea-invaded. Here the limbless torso.

I turned away, only to confront a 'suicide machine'. A young man had made it from packing cases. He wired the trigger of a rifle to a bank of switches and some kind of timing device, then lay down in the machine and waited. Here he was, photographed in his shorts, bloodstains around his head, rigid in his own death-trap. The curator drew my attention to the precautions the young man had taken against staining his landlady's body carpet.

I left the museum having failed to find the disguises, reeling under the impact of what I had seen. The sun-drenched day was filled with menace. Beneath the placid surface of this suburban world, anything was possible. I thought of the Taranaki town in which I had been raised, the rumours of violent death: the adolescent boys who shot their parents as they slept, the lonely farmer who hanged himself in his woolshed, the woman who drowned her moronic son in a swollen creek ... all suppressed by a common conspiracy of silence. Now the truth was out. What had once been kept behind four walls was standing in the outrageous light of day. No censor stood at the gate. Bandages unravelled from suppurating wounds. Grievances, long-buried in the ghetto of the heart, were voiced without apology.

That night I confessed to Les and Mary that I'd taken a bit of a battering by trying to cram too much work into too little time. Driving hundreds of miles to follow up some lead. The stress of talking to strangers. The violence I glimpsed behind our pastoral facades.

The small-town rural New Zealand I had known as a boy had changed. It was far less insular. Less preoccupied with respectability. But while it had become more open to the world, it had lost many of the props which once supported its self-righteous sense of security. The news media purveyed consumerist fantasies – images of a glittering stage where everyone could expect his or her moment of glory. But the stage was overcrowded, and its wings filled with shadows. For the few that might be favoured, thousands were humiliated and spurned. What then of the promise of wealth, of success, that had been held out to them only to be snatched away? Was it chimerical? Refusing to believe that they had been duped by some trick of the light, the losers tore from the hands of whoever stood near them the life that was meant for them alone.

Les heard me out, then gently brought me back to where I had begun.

'What do you think happened to him?' he asked.

I said I didn't know, but mentioned the photo which Joe Pawelka's mother had seen in a newspaper. The group of soldiers in the desert.

If the soldiers were wearing lemon squeezers, Les said, they could have been either New Zealanders or Americans. 'Though the Yanks didn't come into the war until 1917, and they fought only on the Western Front, never in Egypt or the desert.'

'If Pawelka didn't sail from New Zealand but slipped ashore and tried to lose himself, could he have enlisted in the army?' I asked.

'It would have been fairly straightforward,' Les said. 'Compulsory military training began in 1912. He could have enlisted under an assumed name. His lack of a lung would not necessarily have been picked up. He could have volunteered easily in 1 NZEF. Conscription did not get under way until 1916. He would have probably gone to Egypt, then to the Dardanelles.'

Indeed, there is a surviving soldier's letter from Gallipoli which mentions Pawelka. The soldier, who knew Pawelka in the Manawatu, mentions seeing him in the trenches. However, this was probably Joe Pawelka's younger brother Jack who served with the ANZAC force in the Dardanelles before being invalided to England.

As for the mysterious photo, Les said that photos from the front would not have been printed in the dailies. But *The Auckland Weekly News* subscribed to the World Service and ran a four- to eight-page insert in every issue. The photo might have appeared there.

Les went to his study and brought back several photo inserts to show me. They'd been pulled from 1916 issues of *The Auckland Weekly*. One photo was of a group of New Zealand soldiers in Cairo. It was captioned: *MERRY NEW ZEALANDERS LEAVE CAIRO FOR A NEW FIGHTING FRONT: THE MEN, WITH THEIR HATS DECORATED WITH FLOWERS, ABOUT TO TAKE THEIR DEPARTURE FROM AN EGYPTIAN TOWN*. On the facing page were forty-eight photos of New Zealand non-commissioned officers and men 'wounded in the cause of liberty'.

A sobering statistic: 120,000 New Zealand men enlisted in this war: forty-three per cent of men of military age. Of these, 18,500 died in or because of the war, and another 50,000 were wounded.

If Pawelka remained in New Zealand, this may have been his fate. Even if his mother was mistaken about the identity of the soldier in the photo, the fact that she became so preoccupied with it might suggest that Joe had discussed with her the possibility of enlisting. Before his troubles started, he seemed to be attracted to the idea of being in uniform and talked of joining the police. For a man desperate to prove himself, the army might have offered some prospect of redemption. Perhaps he imagined that by some act of heroism he could win back his wife's regard, and even earn himself a pardon from the Crown. He held off writing home, first wanting to make good. But then it was too late ....

In the morning I trudged back to the National Archives. Jack Hansen had been adamant that Joe left Kimbolton on 15 February 1912. Jack's father, Willie, 'knew Joe was bound for Canada'.

I was now determined to try and identify the name under which Joe Pawelka sailed. Figuring that his assumed name would contain some small clue as to his true identity, I began by combing shipping lists.

Unluckily for me, there had been a Genealogical Conference in Wellington during the weekend and many of the participants were now eager to test out their newly acquired research skills. They queued impatiently, with a nervous self-absorption that I found both touching and annoying.

While waiting my turn to place an order, I examined the registry book where researchers had to sign in. Clearly 'family history' had become a compelling subject for Pakeha New Zealanders. People who had set such store by respectability now grubbed about in the shadows of their family trees, assured that enough time had passed to allow some colonial miscreant to be reinvented as a romantic figure.

It was mid-morning when I finally got my hands on the shipping lists for the R.M.S. *Makura* (4920 tons).

The *Makura* sailed from the new Queen Street Wharf, Auckland, at five in the afternoon of 16 February 1912, bound for Vancouver via Suva and Honolulu. Arriving early that same morning from Sydney, the *Makura* loaded a large consignment of butter and hides for Vancouver, as well as ten tons of general cargo for Suva and Honolulu. It carried 246 passengers, 149 of whom embarked in Sydney.

In Auckland that day the wind was fresh and from the south. The afternoon air temperature was 70°F.

My heart was pounding as I scanned the names. On the strength of what Jack had told me about people scraping together money for Joe's fare, I assumed he would not have had a saloon or second-class ticket, so gave my most careful attention to the steerage passengers, fifteen of whom had boarded in Auckland. In the lists, they were designated 'labourers and domestics'. Of the twelve men, one was travelling with his wife. The destination of another, Mr Peterson, was Honolulu. The ten remaining names, written in longhand and difficult to decipher, were these:

Mr H. Neven (?)	Mr A. Collins
Mr R. Russell	Mr H. Gadd
Mr H. Bowker	Mr F. Irving
Mr J. Edge	Mr A. Basich
Mr J. Perrigo	Mr A. Laidlaw

Despite drawing a blank, I decided to photocopy the *Makura* passenger lists, as well as lists for the *Morea* which sailed from Auckland for Sydney and London the same day. Unfortunately, there was, an archival assistant informed me, a 'blanket restriction' on photocopying shipping lists.

I asked if I could speak with the archivist.

I was told it would be a long wait.

With time to kill, I went back to the shipping indexes. When was the next sailing from Auckland?

The *Makura* sailed on Friday. The next sailing was on Monday 19 February. The S.S. *Wimmera* (1871 tons) crossed the Tasman twice a month.

After filing my request for the *Wimmera* passenger lists, I went for lunch.

During the afternoon I worked my way through the names of the steerage passengers on the *Wimmera*. Seventy-six were men. One was a Mr J. Wilson.[3]

I was sure I had tracked him down. He must, I told myself, have had recourse to his second name, John. The thought that he might assume Lizzie's maiden name had already occured to me. But what really clinched the matter was my discovery next day, in the shipping advertisements of *The New Zealand Herald* for February 1912, that tickets purchased for sailings on Union Steam Ship Company boats were interchangeable with Huddart Parker – the company that owned the *Wimmera*.

Was it possible that Joe Pawelka had not sailed for Canada after all? Keeping his plans to himself, had he come to a decision to cover his tracks, cut off all ties with his past, and never look back? When he gave Ted Lawrence the slip in Auckland, was it his intention that no one, not even his family, would know where he was going? As an escaped and hunted criminal, there was no future for him in New Zealand. His wife had washed her hands of him. His family had been obliged to farewell him forever. Under these circumstances, did he choose to die to the life that was now dead to him? Did he turn against the world which he imagined had turned against him, in an act of metaphorical suicide? An act of spite as much as it was an act of survival.

Many of the men who crossed the Tasman in steerage each summer were shearers. Joe Pawelka could have fallen in with them, disembarked in Sydney, gone inland. When war was declared, he may have enlisted. There was a real possibility that he numbered among the thousands of ANZAC casualties at Gallipoli.

But I had no interest in corroborating this scenario. I did not want to pursue J. Wilson any further. I had gone as far as I wanted to go.

With all its horrors, the police museum had been a point of no return. The forensic photos, mug shots and instruments of death had brought home to me how lives get blurred by our clinical descriptions, our pathological labels, our selective fictions. Museums are like morgues or whorehouses. They deal in partial truths. They fetishise fragments of the whole. They hold out the false hope that a shard, a mask, a memento, can spirit a human life back into existence, magically recover its original form.

☙❧

III

The Blind Impress

17

The Remaining Pieces

Back in the States, I worked through the fall and winter on my book and sent what I had written to Jack and Anne. But I told them there were pieces missing from the mosaic, and that these pieces belonged not to the past but to the present.

Jack proposed that when I was next in New Zealand we have 'a round-table conference'. Together with Anne and Helen's children, we would try to 'solve the remaining pieces of the puzzle'.

'Everything,' Jack assured me, 'would sort itself out.'

From Auckland I drove south to Mangaweka, then took the Ruahine road – the same road Joe Pawelka had travelled eighty-three years before – to Kimbolton.

Jack was sitting in his high-backed armchair by a blazing fire, as imperturbable as ever. He was happy to see me and to have another chance to talk. But first a beer.

'What'll you have, Michael?' he asked. 'I've got Tui or DB.'

'I'll take a Tui, Jack. For old times' sake.'

Jack shuffled out into the kitchen, and I followed him. As he took the cans of beer from the fridge, I noticed several bottles of champagne there as well.

We returned to the sitting room, filled our glasses, and drank to each other's health. Bright sunlight filled the window behind Jack's head, blurring the shapes of the furniture in the room.

Jack thanked me for sending him my manuscript. It had helped him understand what I was doing. When I visited him the first time and opened my notebook and started asking questions, he didn't quite know what to make of me.

'You gave a pretty good impression of *not* being mystified!'

'Ah, well, that's water under the bridge.'

I asked about Anne and the others. Did they still intend to come? When would they arrive? Where would they stay? I was concerned that they might want to watch the final race of the America's Cup, which was scheduled for early Sunday morning, and not turn up.

Everything was under control, Jack said. They'd all be here, today or tomorrow. Then he added, 'It's strange that after all these years everything is coming together. It's taken up to the third generation for everyone to get their backsides into gear and do something.'

I asked Jack if he'd mind my asking him a few questions and recording our conversation on tape.

'You go right ahead,' Jack said. 'Ask away.'

I began by asking about Joe's personal effects. Had anything survived?

Jack confessed he had found nothing among his mother's things; Helen's children had inherited Joe's few belongings.

What of the letters Joe had written home when he was a boy? Des Swain had seen them when he was researching his book. Had the letters been in Agnes's possession?

'Not Mum,' Jack said quickly. 'Not Mum. No, no, Swain never met Mum.'

'Oh, really.'

'No, it would have been Helen. Mum was dead before Swain came into it. And I doubt whether Swain would have got past the door if Mum had been alive. She was ... upset ... too much .... I mean, I couldn't go on living with her tears day after day and that sort of thing, you know. I had to vet every blimmin' newspaper before it came into the house, just in case ....'

'It's sad that she never overcame the ....'

'No, no, never. Well, as she'd say, "the shame of it". And yet people just thought the world of her.' Jack sighed.

I asked Jack to tell me something about himself. Had he always lived in the shop, with his mother?

'Oh, yeah, I was a spoiled bugger.'

'Is that why you never married?'

'Possibly.'

'Did you ever come close to it?'

'Oh, yes.'

'I can't believe you didn't have your chances.'

'Well, I don't think I'll die wondering. Put it that way.'

'You never felt like leaving Kimbolton?'

'I was away in the war, you know.'

'After the war?'

'No, I've never regretted the eighty-two years that I've spent here.'

'Never felt isolated ....'

'No. I had my friends. My music.'

'What kind of music?'

'Piano.'

'Did you play and teach?'

'Just played. Oh, yes, I enjoyed entertaining. It gave me great

pleasure and happiness. I had my own orchestra.'
 'What did you call yourselves?'
 'H and P.'
 'For what?'
 'Hansen and Prince.'
 'Who was Prince?'
 'He was a lad from Apiti who played the saxophone. And the drummer boy, he came from Palmerston. If we wanted a fourth one, the double bass came from Palmerston.'
 'Did you just play Saturday nights, or ...?'
 'Played for dances, that sort of thing.'
 I waited for Jack to go on.
 'Then I got very interested in Palmerston Operatic. I played the lead there about four times.'
 'Where did you get your musical gifts?'
 'Mother.'
Jack pointed to the array of photographs on the mantlepiece. 'There's two of the photos of operatic days there,' he said. 'I think Mum's father was quite musical too. Mum said he used to play the cornet.'
 'What instrument did your mother play?'
 'Piano. It was she that got me cracking at playing, too.'
 'Taught you?'
 'Good lord,' Jack exclaimed, examining the back of his hand, 'what have I done to ....'
 'What is it?'
 'I don't know. Must have bumped myself with some wood. Skin's very thin.'
Jack got up and walked stiffly and slowly to the big dining table at the other end of the room. He said he'd dug out some photos I might like to see. But first, how about another beer?
 I said I would get it.

When we'd refilled our glasses, we went over to the table. I stood beside Jack as he showed me the photos.

In the first, taken around the turn of the century, the Pawelka family are outside their cottage in Edwards Street. Joseph sits straight in his chair. One hand is open, the other draws Jack to his side. Agnes stands in the middle of the group, one arm set awkwardly on her father's shoulder. She is holding a wicker basket of fresh flowers. Louisa sits beside her. Joe stands to his mother's right, wearing a bulky serge suit with wide white collar. His arms hang at his sides, his hands loosely cupped.

In poignant contrast, the second photo shows a much older Joseph and Louisa sitting together on deck chairs in their back garden.

Behind them is a corrugated iron water tank and a rank flax bush which has gone to seed. The year is probably around 1920. They are dressed in dark, formal suits. Joseph's beard is grey. His gnarled hands are clasped. Louisa's resolute expression leads one to suspect that she is the stronger of the two, the mainstay of the family, the one who has endured.

This impression is even stronger in another photo of the Hansens and Pawelkas together in the orchard at Edwards Street one Christmas Day in the early 1920s. It is near the end of Joseph's life. He stands alone, face grim, eyes in shadow, knobbly hands with nothing to do. He seems distanced from the others by the stalwart figure of Jack's father, Willie, who faces the camera square on. Willie wears a small bow tie and panama hat. He has a fob watch and chain. His hands are thrust deep into his trouser pockets. He is a picture of confidence, a no-nonsense business man. To his right, shoulder to shoulder, diffidently smiling at the camera, are Agnes, Helen, Jack Pawelka and their mother, as well as Jack Hansen and his half-brother, Ken. Ken has his arms around Jack, and Agnes, kneeling, gazes lovingly at him.

'How old were you that Christmas?' I asked Jack.

'I'd guess eight or nine,' Jack said.

'And that was the orchard at Edwards Street?'

'Louisa loved gardening,' Jack said, and suggested I look at the photo of the house hanging in the passage near his kitchen door.

The photo showed wisteria or clematis clinging to the verandah posts, camellia bushes, and a profusion of European flowers and border plants. No lawns.

Louisa had tended this garden with the same devotion she gave her children. I wondered if she ever thought, pulling weeds, of the biblical parable of the tares.

When I left Jack's place at the end of the afternoon, I drove to Edwards Street and found the open paddock where the Pawelkas' cottage had stood. There were some flax bushes along the fenceline where once a high hedge – shaped as an arch over the front gate – had grown. Three silver birch saplings, tied to stakes, had been planted in the paddock. But there was no vestige of Louisa's garden, neither of the flowers or weeds. Only an empty field with a wind-racked macrocarpa tree beyond it, fretworked against the sky, and the land falling away in great green steps toward the south. When Joseph died in 1923, Louisa and Helen let the cottage and moved to Christchurch. Far from home, Helen found rent-collecting onerous, and it was impossible to maintain the house and garden. The story is told that she came back and burned the house down to collect the insurance money. Perhaps it was also a ritual gesture, reducing to ash the place which had brought her parents such grief. Within the family the story is an ironic commentary on the kinship Helen felt with her long-lost brother. 'Helen and Joe inherited their father's temperament,' Jack said. Agnes and Jack took after their mother. He described Jack Pawelka as 'a fine guy'. 'Tall, dark and handsome; women used to fall for him.' In England during the war he fell in love with a woman whose family regarded him as a poor prospect. Yet she followed Jack out to New Zealand after the war. 'Jack promptly took off to Apia,' Jack said, 'and buried himself there. The Pawelka business stood between them.'

'Did Jack ever marry?'

'Jack left his heart in England. He never married.'

A day before Jack Pawelka died, Jack Hansen flew to Whangarei to see him. He had purchased a plot in the Kimbolton cemetery so that Jack would one day be brought home. But Jack Pawelka did not want to come home, and had specified in his will that he be buried in Whangarei.

As for Helen, she had hardly got to know Joe before he disappeared. But in burning down the family home she symbolically joined herself to him forever.

Only the land remained, until it was taken over in November 1964 by the Ruahine Rabbit Board which paid £300 pounds in compensation to the Pawelka family.

18

Guilt and Shame

I lodged overnight at a bed-and-breakfast place outside Kimbolton and in the morning drove back to Jack's.

As I parked my car in Jack's yard, I could hear starlings lisping and cheeping on the roof of his woodshed. It was a cloudless day, and in the Oroua valley rows of poplars, stripped of their leaves, stood like bundles of faggots, furled.

Jack had the fire blazing, and the TV turned on for the America's Cup. On the tea trolley were champagne glasses ready to be filled.

But it was neither Team New Zealand nor the prospect of the America's Cup 'coming home' that Jack wanted to celebrate, but the reunion of the family. As far as today was concerned, he said, the sun was already over the yard-arm.

It wasn't long before Anne arrived, bustling into the room with files and folders. Then John and Fay – Helen's children – turned up with their spouses. They, too, had brought boxes of photos, genealogies and family memorabilia.

Jack introduced me and ordered another bottle of Marque Vue sparkling wine uncorked.

When our glasses were charged, Jack said: 'This drink is to having the family together for the first time in a long, long while.'

Though my research had been the catalyst for our meeting, Joe Pawelka did not dominate it. For Joe's nephews and niece, clearing up the mystery of his disappearance eighty-three years ago was far less urgent than the affirmation of their survival as a family. John, Fay, Jack and Anne had met separately but never together. Now, as they began to share their photos and memorabilia, the talk was less of Joe than of Agnes and Helen, who had struggled to escape his shadow. It was a struggle John and Fay had also experienced.

At primary school in Kimbolton, Fay remembered how kids used to taunt her in the playground:

> One, two, three, four
> Joe Pawelka jumped the wall.

She recalled some of her mother's memories. Of when she was eight and came home from school at lunchtime with a friend one day to find Joe in the kitchen with Louisa. Of the police poking pitchforks into the haystack behind the house, but too afraid to go into the hayshed lest Joe was hiding there.

But mostly Helen said nothing of her brother.

'Any time I mentioned the name Pawelka, the walls came up,' John said.

'She felt shame,' John's wife, Maria, added. 'It ruined her life. You can't imagine what it was like back then. Joe's brother Jack never married because he carried the Pawelka name. He didn't want his children to be stigmatised by having to carry it too.'

'When Jack was working for the post office they wanted him to change his name,' Jack said. 'But he refused.'

'We were never allowed to mention his name,' Fay said. 'Mum didn't keep some of the things she got from Louisa. She destroyed a lot of things that had to do with Joe. She was ashamed of the memory.'

When she was eighty-seven, Agnes wrote her nephew about a television film that was being made about her brother. She said: 'When Joe disgraced us, we lost touch with everyone, thinking they would not want to have anything more to do with us. I suppose we were too sensitive; and now it's all going to be dragged up again in a film. I wish God I was dead and out of it. There is no doubt about the innocent having to suffer for the guilty unto the third or fourth generation. People are so cruel ....'

Toward the end of 1936, *The Weekly News* commissioned an article on Joe Pawelka and prepared to publish an updated account of the events of 1910. Jack Pawelka was sent the proofs. He at once despatched an angry letter to Sir Henry Horton, owner of the newspaper, insisting that the article not be published. Jack must have told his mother about the article too, because she wrote Horton with the same request.

John showed me the telegram which Sir Henry Horton sent Louisa on 23 January 1937:

SINCERELY REGRET HAVING CAUSED YOU ANY DISTRESS PUBLICATION WITHHELD IN DEFERENCE TO YOUR REQUEST

Twelve days later, the editor of *The Weekly News* wrote Jack Pawelka. The letter, addressed to Mr John Pawelka, Telegraph Office, Whangarei, and dated 4 February 1937, began:

> *Dear Sir,*
> *Sir Henry Horton has passed over to me your letter relating to the proposed publication of a new account of the Pawelka case. Naturally we do not wish to do anyone an injustice but I would*

> *ask you to consider this point of view as it appears to me. None of Joseph Pawelka's relatives are accused of anything. They have nothing to be ashamed of.*

The editor misses the point. For the Pawelkas, the question of Joe's *guilt* is not the issue, but rather the family's *shame*. Joe was still a wanted man. Though Joseph Senior had died in 1923, Louisa and her children feared the legal repercussions of having helped Joe evade justice. Sheltering him in Kimbolton during the summer of 1911–1912 and siding with him against the state had implicated the family in his crimes. And underscoring this was the deeply held conviction that Joe was their flesh and blood. Louisa embraced the Catholic Moravian notion that the blood-bond between mother and child was like the bond between self and God. Whatever one did in one's life would bring not only divine retribution or reward, but curse or bless every member of one's family. A bad seed or black sheep could condemn his or her family to shame, and reciprocally, abandonment by the family could spell a person's ruin. Joe's guilt thus became his family's remorse. If he was written off as a lunatic, they shared the stigma. And as they shrank from the world, driven in upon themselves and their own spiritual resources, Joe's tragic fate only intensified their already fierce sense of unity and loyalty. Just as a death or birth may transcend bitter differences between a parent and a child, so Joe's loss deepened the bond between Louisa, Joseph and their errant son. And it is out of this intense and inescapable kinship that the sense of shame is born. The family had endured a wrong and suffered a loss that no absolution or pardon could make good. The Pawelkas bore this terrible sense of difference as a sense of being marked and stained. It was a loss of face. A humiliation. A disgrace. Nothing could ever heal the wounds. Lizzie might revert to her maiden name, but the child she bore would always be the embodiment of her union with the Pawelkas. The families into which the other Pawelka children married were just as profoundly affected; both the Hansens and Bryces bore the Pawelkas' loss in sympathy and solidarity. As for the Wilsons, they too suffered the same stigma. In a conversation with one descendant, I would be told, 'The oldies tried to keep the shame of the relationship between Joe and Lizzie from the kids. And the children of that generation kept mum for years. As youngsters growing up, everything was hush-hush in the family. Mum, as a young girl of nine or ten, took a lot of flak because of her relationship to him. She had to run the gauntlet past the Catholic school. Kids would taunt her about being related to a murderer and thief.'*

For the Pawelkas, nothing could bring Joe back. Nothing could rewrite the past or rectify the tragic flaw. The family could only hope to dull its pain by distraction or forgetting. As Jack put it, Joe's father 'took to the grog', while Louisa 'took to the garden and her rosary beads'.

Despite adversity, Louisa kept a faithful record of every rite of passage in the life of the family.

When Fay showed me Louisa's prayer-book, it was like being given a glimpse into the family's soul.

The small, battered Catholic missal measured about three inches by five. The boards were covered in purple cloth. There was a tarnished metal cross on the front cover. The binding was broken. I had to turn the dog-eared, age-blotched, brittle pages with care.

In several pages in the front and back of the book, Louisa had, over the years, written details of births, deaths and marriages. Here

---

* Coincidentally, Marion Leahy (née Wilson), who shared these reminiscences with me, was the granddaughter of Sarah Wilson (née Spinks) who lived three doors from my grandparents' place. When telling me about Joe Pawelka, my grandfather would often mention 'old Mrs Wilson who lives along the street', but it wasn't until I met Marion Leahy that I learned of her exact connection with Joe Pawelka. Sarah Wilson married James Wilson, one of Lizzie's older brothers. James Wilson died in 1944; Sarah eighteeen years later in 1962.

was the date of her arrival in New Zealand and of her marriage to Joe Senior when she still called herself Louise König. Here were the birthdays of her sons, Joseph John Thomas (Joe) and John Alfred (Jack) and of her daughters Agnes and Florence Helen. Here also were the dates on which her children left home.

One page arrested me. Though the right-hand edge of the page was tattered, making it impossible to decipher two of the dates, here at last was confirmation of the date of Joe's final leave-taking. His name, Joseph John Thomas, was reduced to initials, possibly to disguise a potentially incriminating fact.

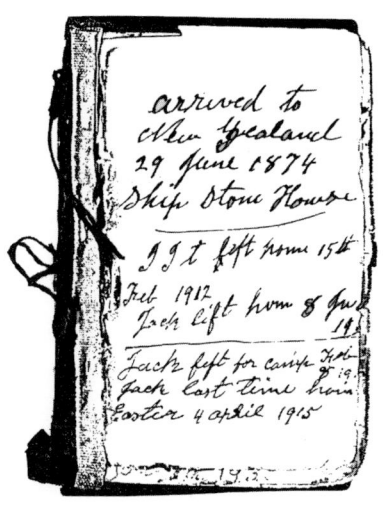

J.J.T left home 15th Feb 1912

A later entry reads:

Joe left home 15th Feb 1912

'She wrote him out of her life,' Jack said.

I noticed that Louisa had also noted the date Joe's daughter, Iris, was born, as well as the year Lizzie died. It showed the depth of Louisa's belief in the integrity and continuity of the family. Equally significant were the recycled names, such as Joseph and John, and evidence of Louisa's efforts to maintain the link with Joseph Senior's North Canterbury kin and all their in-laws.

I was especially interested in Louisa's contacts with the Wilsons. 'Did Louisa see anything of Lizzie and Iris?' I asked Jack.

'Oh yes, after the initial meeting the two grandmothers were more or less friendly. They kept in touch with each other.'

Iris's birth had begun the healing process. In July 1910, Lizzie's mother, Hannah, sent a picture postcard from Ashhurst to Louisa in Kimbolton. On one side of the card was a scene of the jetty at Day's Bay, Wellington. On the other:

> *Just a line to tell you that Lizzie (Mrs Pawelka) has a fine little girl born on the 23rd inst. Hope to see you down.*
>
> H.A. Wilson

Perhaps Hannah Wilson was moved to console Louisa for the loss of her son. Perhaps the birth of Iris did transcend the tragedy which Joe had brought upon the two families.

On 3 October the following year, five weeks after Joe's escape from prison, Louisa telephoned Lizzie and asked if they could meet. A rendezvous was arranged for the next day in a Palmerston North tea-room.

Inevitably, Lizzie was accompanied by her mother.

Louisa asked Lizzie if she could ever forgive Joe. She showed Lizzie a letter Joe had written, in which he swore he had not killed McGuire and had not been solely responsible for stealing the furniture. Joe argued that because his accomplice was married and had children, he could not stop him. But he wanted to see his daughter and urged Lizzie to forgive him and go with him to another country where they could make a fresh start.

Lizzie was so distressed by the letter that Hannah took it from her and would not give it back.

Louisa then asked Lizzie if she would at least write to Joe.

But her appeals fell on deaf ears. Finally, Louisa asked if she could hold the baby and perhaps go out onto the street with her for a few minutes?

Lizzie said no. 'She was terrified that the old lady was going to kidnap the babe,' Jack said.

As Louisa got up to go, she implored the Wilsons not to tell anyone that they had met. But two days later, Lizzie gave a full report of the meeting to Constable Watts at Ashhurst, asking Watts to exercise discretion because she was afraid of what Joe might do if he got wind of what she had divulged.

When Sergeant Bowden interviewed Jack's father, Willie, a week after the meeting between Lizzie and Louisa in Palmerston North, Willie asserted that the Pawelkas 'are now reconciled to Mrs Pawelka and child, and that the elder Mrs Pawelka has visited her daughter-in-law and grandchild at Ashhurst several times.' But, he noted: 'The grandmother is anxious that her daughter-in-law let her have the child but she will not part with it, the friends of the family would also like Mrs Pawelka and child to leave Ashhurst ....'

Iris Wilson, four years old.

Lizzie's fear was, in part, clearly a reaction to Louisa's suggestion that she give up her child to the Pawelkas.

'Did they ever meet again?'

'Oh, yes, regularly, I think, when Iris grew up.'

Anne showed me a photo that had been taken by the fountain in the Palmerston North Square sometime in the early '30s. Iris, Louisa and Lizzie are sitting on the concrete edge of the fountain. Iris is flanked by her mother and mother-in-law. She is wearing a fashionable coat with fur trim, a hat and gloves. Louisa's face communicates resolution and forbearance. In her dark suit, shirt and striped tie, Lizzie looks as dour as the principal of a girls' church boarding school.

The room was filled with cigarette smoke. The blazing fire and sunlight pouring through the window made it almost unbearably hot. And we had been drinking sparkling wine steadily for three hours. My head spinning, I took in the empty glasses and bottles, the photographs and papers littered on the table, piano, tea trolley, and chair arms, and the wedgewood saucers on the maple-leaf wallpaper ....

'Time for lunch,' Maria declared.

She and Fay had made tomato and cheese sandwiches and prepared plates of sliced venison. Fay's husband, Wayne, refilled my glass.

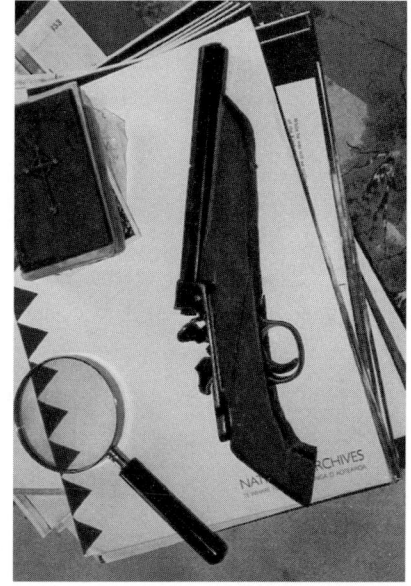

Jack wanted me to be sure I saw everything. That I copied everything. Fortunately, there was a photocopier in the shop. I had only to open the door behind my chair and it was two steps away. So I made copies of papers and photos at every opportunity and scribbled down as much of the conversation as discretion permitted. I took a photograph of Louisa's missal placed beside a magnifying glass and Joe's revolver. The revolver had been found in the family cottage in Edwards Street, Jack said. He kept it for many years, but when Agnes died Helen took it to Wanganui. Joe must have made the revolver himself, when he was a boy. It was a sawn-off .22 rifle. The bevelled barrel bore the patent mark of H. Pieper's, Liege, Belgium. Joe had fashioned a wooden stock for it. It brought home to me that Joe had loved firearms from an early age. And was a crack shot.

'Frankly,' Jack said, 'what are we going to do with it? Give it to Anne, or to the Police Museum? What do you think, John?'

Jack had given other things to Anne. He wanted her to have something of the inheritance her mother had kept from her. He had sent her old photos, to help the bridge the gap between her and Joe.

But what of the photo of the soldiers – the one in which Louisa thought she had identified Joe?

Fay said that according to Helen, Joe had promised to send his mother a newspaper as a way of letting her know he was well. The photo did not come through the mail. Louisa saw it in a newspaper. 'It was a picture of some Canadian servicemen,' Fay said.

'The mother said, "That looks like my son," ' Jack added.

'For a guy who loved his mother, he would have taken every opportunity to communicate,' Anne said.

'I'll never forgive him for not getting in touch with his mother,' Jack said.

'If he was dead, how could he have got in touch?' Anne rejoined.

Fay said she had consulted a Ouija board – not something she would ordinarily do – to find out what happened to Joe. The Ouija board gave her to understand that Joe had died at sea.

After lunch, I went up to the cemetery with Anne, John, Maria and Fay. The day was warm and still. I sat on a gravestone, looking out over the Oroua valley to the blue range of the Ruahines, while John and Fay went around identifying the Bryce and Pawelka plots. Then we returned to Jack's place, where everyone began packing up and preparing to leave. For Jack, the reunion had been momentous. Calling me Mike and 'young chap', he said, 'It's been a great day. It won't happen again.' Anne thanked me for bringing them all together.

Florence Helen's children John Bryce and Fay Jaquiery at Kimbolton Cemetery, May 1995.

Anne Harris at Kimbolton Cemetery, May 1995.

But as I drove away from Kimbolton, I felt suddenly bereft. I thought of staying another night, seeing Jack again. But then told myself that it would be better to see him in a week's time, when I had done what I wanted to do in the National Archives. So I headed south along the Kimbolton Road in dwindling light, thinking of the night Joe cycled furiously down the same road after escaping from the police ambush in Edwards Street.

At the bridge over the Kiwitea Stream on the outskirts of Feilding, I stopped to take photos of the shingle banks and scrub where Joe was seen next morning. I drove down Derby Street to East Street and on to Aorangi, taking the route he had taken to avoid the centre of town.

At the corner of Aorangi and Cameron's Line there is a choice: to continue straight on toward Bunnythorpe and Ashhurst or turn west toward Awahuri. I wondered if Joe Pawelka had hesitated. These forking paths. His wife in Ashhurst. A friend in Awahuri perhaps, or beyond in Longburn, who might shelter him.

Should I drive to Ashhurst, take a look at the Wilson house at the corner of Salisbury and Wyndham Streets, or head toward Awahuri where Joe was arrested?

It was getting dark. I took the road he took.

೮೩೮೦

19

Death's Secretary

The idea recurs: our lives are storied. Were it not for stories, our lives would be unimaginable; we could not make sense of the times we live. Stories make it possible for us to overcome our separateness, to find common ground and common cause.

To relate a story is to retrace one's steps, going over the ground of one's life again, reworking reality to render it more bearable. A story enables us to fuse the world without and the world within. In this way we gain some purchase over events that confounded us, humbled us, left us helpless. In telling a story we renew our faith that the world is within our grasp.

Any story is like a vessel shaped from wet clay under a potter's hands. In its roundedness, containedness and completeness it provides the consoling illusion that life has meaning. And just as a clay vessel bears tell-tale traces of the potter's hands, so too, Walter Benjamin observes, every story carries the personal imprint of the storyteller.

Consider the stories occasioned by Joe Pawelka's life.

A psychotherapist might discern in the circumstances of Joe Pawelka's childhood, in his recorded remarks, and in his behaviour under stress, a picture of clinical narcissism. Convinced that fate has singled him out as a victim of injustice, this individual will do anything to draw attention to himself. To this end, heroism and notoriety, affection and contempt, are on a par. Deep down he remains a resentful child who thinks he deserves to be pandered, and when the going gets rough appeals to others for rescue and care. Thus the overweening and remorseless need for acceptance. The habits of feigned illness and sham dementia. The threats of suicide, the manipulative confabulations, the downright lies. Such aggressive narcissism is an attempt to bend the world to one's will. One's sole reality is one's own needs, one's own feelings, one's own state of mind. By contrast, the world of others is weightless and colourless; affectively does not exist.

There may be grains of truth in this picture. But it is only a picture – underexposed and poorly developed.

What of the juridical story?

At Waikanae, I spoke to Stewart Lusk, a retired Q.C. who had become interested in the Pawelka case when researching his history of Kimbolton.

Stewart Lusk was convinced an injustice had been done: 'The judge got it wrong, no doubt about that. Judges in those days had enormous power.'

In the charge of murder, ballistic evidence was inconclusive. In the case of arson at the Palmerston Boys' High School, it is arguable that the techniques of fingerprinting which proved Pawelka's guilt were, in 1910, somewhat fallible. On other counts, the prosecution's evidence was circumstantial, and there is reasonable doubt in the cases of some of the crimes Pawelka was charged with. One has only to read police reports from the period when he was hiding at Kimbolton to see how things were stacked against him. In a report dated 9 September 1911, Sub-Inspector Norwood listed several 'incidents' in his police district, including a breaking and entering at Tokomaru, a 'mysterious fire' at Longburn, a suspicious camp site at Awapuni, the theft of food from a house in Palmerston, and an attempt to force an entry to Swallow's Booksellers adjoining premises owned by Pawelka's 'uncle' in Palmerston. Norwood drew this conclusion: 'The depredation's referred to may have been committed by any criminal but the methods are, I am informed, similar to those adopted by Pawelka when he was last at large in this district.' The irony was that even as Norwood wrote these lines, Joe Pawelka was positively identified near Mt Messenger in Taranaki!

Of all the stories which invoke fact; perhaps none are more tenacious than newspaper stories. Written in the confident if naïve belief that 'getting the facts right' will also settle the attendant moral, legal and political issues, such stories quickly take on a life of their own.

When *The Weekly News* commissioned its article on Joe Pawelka in 1936, the rationale was that the facts be given precedence over personal sensibilities and possible slights. Thus, despite assuring Louisa that the story had been killed, the editor defended his right to publish it. Writing to Jack Pawelka, he argued: 'I can understand your unwillingness to have the case needlessly re-opened to go over the facts as they have been published before, but I would point out to you that the author has had full access to police and other records and has gone to great trouble with his story with the object of doing your brother justice. Surely Joseph Pawelka has a right to have his name cleared. There is no shame for his family in this.'

The editor went on to stress that the public was fascinated by the Pawelka story, and he urged Jack Pawelka to appreciate the need to have 'the facts put straight' in 'the interests of pure history'.

The Pawelka family rejected this argument, and fifty years later was still opposed to the idea of raking over dead coals.

In 1987, broadcaster and freelance journalist Des Swain began his research on Joe Pawelka and met with the same resistance.

In a letter to Iris McGaffin – Joe's and Lizzie's daughter – whom he had traced through a birth certificate, marriage records, and the electoral roles, Swain sought to mollify her by painting a flattering portrait of Joe and pointing out that he could not have killed McGuire and did not shoot to kill Pauline Kendall. Testifying to the 'positive aspects of his character', Swain wrote: 'I am satisfied that a large number of comments about Joe Pawelka had no basis in fact: that he was a much better man than people are led to believe.'

Iris was elderly and ill when she received Swain's letter. Not wanting to confront the spectre of the past, she did not reply. But her son Terry wrote John Bryce, suggesting he contact Swain. Terry made one stipulation: 'Mum requests that you do not involve the newer generation, i.e. her children and grandchildren.'

Des Swain dubbed his book an 'historical novel'. Unabashedly sympathetic to his protagonist, Swain makes Joe Pawelka a tragic hero. At the end of his book, touching on Joe's disappearance, he writes: 'I cannot for a moment imagine that Joe would not have let his family know when he was safe.'

> As the *Makura* pulled out of the Waitemata, out of the Hauraki Gulf, and the darkness started to come down, what were his thoughts as he watched the water slide past the bow?
>
> He said he would sooner die than go to gaol. He was going to irrevocable exile; he was leaving New Zealand for the first time; he would never see the gentle Louisa or the family again; his marriage had ended; the one woman he still loved had rejected him; he had never seen, would never see, his child.
>
> The water must have looked welcoming.

Reading this scenario, I did not weep for Joe, as Swain did. Nor did I feel inclined to thank Joe Pawelka, as Swain was moved to do, 'for showing us something of who we are: of celebrating humanity'. But this kind of romantic myth-making dies hard.

Not long after Des Swain began work on his 'historical novel', Anne Harris learned of her kinship with Joe Pawelka. And the story she came to tell was also steeped in romanticism. 'I'm a terrible romantic,' Anne told me. 'Lizzie and Joe must have been so in love.' In Anne's view Joe couldn't do enough for his young bride, but had very little money, 'so when he had a chance to acquire some inexpensive furniture he jumped at it.' Anne was aware that this was very likely *not* what happened. 'It's my theory,' she said. 'It's based on the sort of thing I'd do.'

For Joe's parents and siblings, such heroic nostalgia would have been as futile as the argument of the editor of *The Weekly News*: that proving Joe innocent of the violent crimes of which he was accused would alleviate his descendants' shame and stigma. The fact is, however, that for Joe's immediate family there was no redemptive myth.

While Rosina may have told herself that Joe's tragic life was divine retribution for his parents' heedlessness, Louisa and Joseph could never bring their son's story to a close. It had a beginning, a middle, but no end ... though Louisa may have imagined some God-given resolution in the afterlife. Until their own deaths ended their self-questioning, they kept their silence and implored others to do the same. For the children's sake. In the hope that in forgetfulness and the fullness of time their pain might ease.

What then of the story I had written?

John Berger observes that 'any story drawn from life begins, for the storyteller, with its end'. Most stories, he goes on to say, 'begin with the death of the principal protagonist. It is in this sense that one can say that storytellers are Death's secretaries. It is Death who hands them the file.'

At Jack's 'round table' in Kimbolton I had been a ghostly eavesdropper, registering a story which at times brought tears, at other times laughter. But though I was privy to these unrehearsed recollections and shared memories, I was an outsider. Almost a voyeur.

What had brought us together? And why now?

Our meeting had little to do with vindicating Joe. If anything, it was a celebration of being free of his legacy. Greater than any sense of his presence was the sense of Helen's absence. If shame is a kind of perpetual grieving, then the family, working through their grief over Helen's death, had at last begun to unburden itself of the shame it had shared with her.

Helen had been the last of Joe's generation. 'An afterthought,' Fay said. Much younger than the others, she was the last to have known Joe in life. Though Jack liked to tell me that if Helen had been alive my research would have been easier, I knew that it would have been harder, because I, like the others, would have been bound by the same taboo against talking about the past – the sole defence Helen and the others had against further hurt. The generosity with which John and Fay showed me Helen's heirlooms, and confided to me what they remembered of her and Joe, expressed their freedom from an old constraint.

But this was only my guess. For Jack and the others, our meeting was a mystery. 'It's strange that after all these years everything is coming together,' he had told me, 'like Barbara getting in touch at the same time that you got onto the story.'

But as soon as we tried to clear up the mystery, we found ourselves again standing in Joe's long shadow.

Anne was convinced that Joe's spirit had brought us together. John's wife, Maria, agreed. Joe's spirit had presided over our meeting.

It was Joe who inspired Barbara Blyth (née Pavelka) to contact the others last year. And it had been Joe who had moved me to write my book.

George Santayana once observed that those who cannot remember the past are condemned to repeat it. But what is the point of remembering the past unless it helps us get beyond the situation that has shaped the way we are?

Overshadowing the spadework of the scholar are the claims of the living. The limits placed on what we may know of Joe Pawelka are not fixed by the paucity of the evidence as to his character, his guilt, or his ultimate fate. They are set by the exigencies of the time and place in which we live.

Forays into the past are justified, I like to think, only when the past gives us some guidelines for how we can live less divisively and more generously in the here and now.

❦

20

Stories Happen

After a final trip to Wellington, I went back to see Jack one more time. I told him that I had come to realise that there was a curious symmetry between Joe's story and my story about his story. Researching his life and times had brought me home. Not to the place I left thirteen years ago, but to a place where I wanted to make a new start. Ironically, in trying to make sense of Joe's disaffection, I had recovered a sense of my own belonging, my own turangawaewae. Joe's loss had become my gain.

'So everything's come full circle,' Jack said.

The air was clear and cold. I heard only the sound of my feet on the road. Then, in the distance, on another road, a car changed gears, went on, and diminished into the hills.

When I heard the next car, I did not bother to turn. It sped by, scattering leaves, then stopped fifty yards ahead and waited.

I hurried toward it. I could see the driver observing me in his rear-view mirror.

He was in his seventies. He shaded his eyes when he asked where I was going.

'Auckland,' I said.

He said he could take me some of the way.

I opened the passenger door and threw in my grip. There was a Pekinese dog on the back seat. The dog got up on its front legs, sniffed the air, and settled back to sleep.

'You're American,' I said.

'Can you see smoke?' he asked, ignoring my remark. 'Or is that steam?'

'It looks like your radiator's boiling over.'

'Can't be. It's a new car. Hasn't even done 5,000 miles.'

When I suggested we take a look, he seemed reluctant. I had to ask him to unlock the hood. He stayed behind the wheel while I lifted and propped it.

Water and steam were sputtering from the uncapped radiator. I could see the cap. It was lodged against the crankcase. I reached down and got it between my fingers, and extracted it gingerly. Then I walked around to the driver's window and told him I would go and get some water to top up the radiator.

'Where are you going to get water out here?'

I said I'd take care of it, and set off back down the road to the house I'd walked past minutes before, at the end of a long drive, half hidden by a belt of macrocarpas.

A woman let me borrow a watering can. I unscrewed the rose and went to the water tank behind the house. There was a muddy depression and downtrodden grass where some kids had been puddling around. I straddled the mud hole and filled the can.

When I got back to the car, the American was smoking a cigarette and seemed unconcerned that he'd come close to blowing up his engine.

'OK,' I said. 'Start her up.'

He switched on and slowly I filled the radiator. Then I secured the cap, slammed the hood and got back in the car.

'You wouldn't mind driving, would you?' he said.

'That's fine with me,' I said.
'I'm not so used to driving on the wrong side of the road.'
So we swapped places.

After returning the watering can, I accelerated onto the highway. It was a powerful car and easy to drive. I felt at peace with myself. I had hitched this highway for more than thirty years. Every stretch and bend in the road was part of an unfolding story, and every time I travelled the road another chapter was added. Yet the stories were as randomly connected as the lives of those who had given me lifts over the years, or the makes of the vehicles they drove.

For several miles the American said little. Then, passing through Taihape, he said, out of the blue, that it looked like a lonely sort of place to have to spend one's life.

I had no idea what to say to this. But it didn't matter. He followed up the remark by asking me if I was aware that the war had ended fifty years ago.

I had to admit that I hadn't really given it much thought.

'I guess it was before your time,' he said.

He had enlisted in Brooklyn in 1941. Within a year he was with the Marines at Guadalcanal.

'You think thirteen's unlucky,' he said. 'Well, it was Friday the 13th. Our destroyer was 13th in the line. Our ship's number was 445 ... that's thirteen if you add it up ... and our Task Force number was 67 ... thirteen again.'

He was afraid. In the darkness off Guadalcanal, the sea was like glass. The destroyer's bow wave shimmered with phosphorescence, and the cloying air was filled with the hothouse fragrance of night-blooming tropical flowers.

'To this day, I can't go into a florist's shop without it getting the better of me. In Wellington, I wanted to buy my daughter some flowers, but I couldn't. How about that? I had to take her a box of chocolates.'

Then the night exploded with salvos from the destroyer's five-inch guns and retaliative fire from the Japanese battle line. He was in the pilothouse. It filled with a reddish light, and a bolt of hot air concussed the ship. The destroyer ahead had blown up.

They ploughed through burning oil. He felt sick with horror at the thought of the men in the water they might be running through. He saw Japanese torpedoes pass beneath them. The sky was on fire. Star shells. Rocket clusters. Parachute flares. Oil was burning on the surface of the sea.

He remembers men cursing the bulky life-jackets which hampered their movements on the bridge. Then came the sound of an incoming shell, like a bed sheet being ripped down the middle.

He felt himself hurtling through the mouth of a furnace. There were screams. Screaming inside his head. Then he saw that he was on fire.

'When they got me out, I looked like a cheese melt on a piece of burned toast.'

Suffering from burns and a leg shattered by shrapnel, he was flown to Australia. For weeks he lay immobilised in the base hospital at Townsville, oppressed by homesickness.

'I kept remembering Brooklyn. Brooklyn, Brooklyn, nothing but Brooklyn. Night and day. I guess I was lucky, though. Lucky thirteen, huh? At least I got out in one piece.'

While convalescing, he had a fling with an Australian nurse. 'I didn't know it at the time, but I put her in the family way.' He went back to his unit, forgot the nurse and presumed she had forgotten him. 'She probably saw herself as a casualty of the war, like me, and left it at that.'

'It's a strange thing, memory. I can never forget that smell of gardenias off Guadalcanal. Never forget my buddies. Things like this are more vivid to me than this morning's coffee. But I can't remember her ....'

Waiouru was behind us. To the west the mountains were in cloud. A soft rain was beginning to fall.

'I wouldn't want you to think I am a man completely without qualities,' he said at last, 'but memory's a strange thing. 'Specially in wartime.'

'I've seen photos of her now. I still can't make the photos fit with anything I remember. I guess she didn't want to go crying over spilled milk. Never wanted to bother me. She had her child. A daughter. Raised her there in Townsville. Told her all about me. At least as much as she knew.

'The daughter never saw any point in going back into the past, either. It was her husband started looking for me. He convinced her she should know who her father was. You know, before it was too late ....'

'Is she in Australia?'

'No. Lives here. In Wellington. That's where I've been. Her husband's a Kiwi.'

'How did they find you?'

'Talk about luck. I tell you. She knew my name, right, because her mother remembered it. She even remembered I was a Brooklyn boy. So the daughter and her husband place advertisements in the Personals in the New York dailies. Then they get hold of New York telephone directories and start phoning up everyone with my name. Finally they get through to a nephew of mine, and he tells them I'm living in L.A. So we start exchanging letters. Before long, the whole thing gets too much for me. What the hell, I say to my wife. What have I got to lose? So I come out here to meet her.'

He paused. 'It didn't work out. We were strangers. What can you expect? Life's not in the business of happy endings. But I tell you, I was real excited for awhile, coming all the way out here. I was going to reconnect with something I lost. Like getting in a time machine ....'

'She gave me the dog. She and her husband breed them. A memento, she said, to remind you of Mum. So I'm taking Memento back to the States next week. My wife likes dogs. I don't much care for them. And the quarantine's going to be hell for the poor little tyke. But my wife's got a soft spot for animals. She'll give it a home.'

I was tired and famished. I needed a break from driving and from this relentless story. I wished I'd suggested stopping at Waiouru. Now, with the ashen landscape surrounding us, all tussock and hebe and mist, I knew it would be another half-hour before we got to Turangi.

But the Ancient Mariner wasn't perturbed. His daughter had packed some sandwiches for him. They were in the trunk of the car. Why not pull off the road somewhere. He wasn't hungry, but he could go a cup of coffee.

I stopped near Oturere Bridge. The beech trees were blackened with rain. But we were out of the wind, and the damp air smelled of moss and mountain water.

The American let his dog out for a run around. It scampered away into the flax and toi toi.

We sat at a picnic table and unpacked the sandwiches. He poured two cups of coffee from his Thermos flask. I wondered, now that his story was finished, whether he would want to take over the driving. Perhaps he'd want to be alone now, with his thoughts. I considered leaving him there with his dog and catching another ride.

But he was not done.

He wanted to tell me about his Guardian Angel. He wanted to tell me the story of his three failed marriages. He wanted to show me photos of his house at Marina del Rey, to impress upon me how lucky he'd been to buy it before real estate went through the roof. He wanted to talk about his annual reunion in Brooklyn with his war buddies.

So we continued, with the lake coming into view under clearing skies.

He had talked for two hours without flagging. Now, as his monologue turned to trout fishing, I glanced in the rear-view mirror at the weather closing in behind us. Then, for some reason, I tilted the mirror so I could see the dog on the back seat.

'Is your daughter's dog on the floor?' I asked.

He turned in a panic. The dog was neither on the seat nor the floor. The dog was still sniffing around the toi toi and flax by the Oturere Stream. We had forgotten to get it back into the car before driving off.

I stopped the car on the dirt track that ran beside the lake.

'We'll go back for it,' I said.

'I'll go back. You don't have to come.'

'But if you hadn't picked me up, you wouldn't have forgotten your dog.'

'It's not your fault, pal. I should've checked.'

'You sure?'

'Sure, I'm sure. You go on. You've got a family waiting for you. You get back to them.'

I got out of the car. How did he know I had a family?

As I stood and watched, he turned back onto the highway and headed south into the murky weather over the volcanic plateau to look for his daughter's dog.

I went down to the lake. I wanted to record as much as I could of what he had said.

Later, when I got to thinking about it, I realised that the ending to Joe Pawelka's story could never be the ending I had originally sought.

Time was not a white line down the middle of a strip of bitumen, with a determinate point of departure and a final destination. Time warps and buckles and folds back upon itself, bringing the present into intimate contact with the distant past, and making successive moments seem a lifetime apart.

If time is a river, it is a river that does not run its course straightforwardly to the sea. There are whirlpools, eddies, oxbows, falls, backwaters and counter-currents. Periodically the river overflows its banks, obliterating the line between land and water, changing its course entirely.

Endings, like beginnings, are misnomers. Listen to the river. It fills the night. Listen to our lives, as they replay the same piece of music in infinite variations.

Clouds were being tumbled across the sky. The lake water was breaking on the black shingle. As I wrote, the wind flicked the pages of my notebook against the back of my hand.

◦₃₈◦

The Blind Impress

Acknowledgements

I acknowledge with love my wife Francine and my first-born daughter Heidi – my mainstays in troubled times. I would also like to thank Juliet Batten, Les and Mary Cleveland, Bryn and Isabelle Jones, Judith Loveridge and Keith Ridler, Bronwen Nicholson and Brian Boyd, Jennifer Shannon and Allan Thomas for their unfailing friendship and hospitality to me in New Zealand. For their generous help and goodwill, I owe a great deal to John and Maria Bryce, Ray Carter, Jack Hansen, Anne Harris, Richard Hill, Desmond Hurley, Fay Jaquiery, Stewart Lusk and Marion Leahy. Acknowledgement is also made for permission to quote materials from the following sources:

National Archives, Wellington: **Police Department File** 1910 on Escaped Prisoner John Joseph Pawelka (National Archives, P1 1910/610); **Criminal Record Book** No. 11 of the Magistrates Court, Palmerston North, covering the period 5 May 1909 to 25 October 1910 (National Archives, Box 855 AAOY W 3298); **Trial and Sentencing File:** Rex versus Joseph John Pawelka, Supreme Court of NZ, Palmerston North (National Archives, Box 734 AAOY W3298); **Passenger Lists**, Auckland outward, Jan–July 1912 (National Archives SS 1 311). Alexander Turnbull Library, Wellington: *The Manawatu Evening Standard, The New Zealand Truth, The Evening Post* and *The New Zealand Times.*

Photo Sources

page 19	I.B. Mandahl Ltd.
page 23	Anne Harris
page 37	Marion Leahy
page 38	Marion Leahy
page 40	Alexander Turnbull Library
page 50	Alexander Turnbull Library
page 50	Alexander Turnbull Library
page 51	I.B. Mandahl Ltd.
page 51	I.B. Mandahl Ltd.
page 52	Alexander Turnbull Library
page 54	Albert William Organ (1912)
page 59	Alexander Turnbull Library
page 69	Albert William Organ (1912)
page 100	Marion Leahy
page 122	Michael Jackson
page 138	Marion Leahy
page 139	Anne Harris
page 157	Marion Leahy
page 158	Anne Harris
page 159	Jack Hansen
page 161	Jack Hansen
page 169	Anne Harris
page 170	Anne Harris
page 171	Michael Jackson
page 173	Michael Jackson
page 173	Michael Jackson

Notes

page 12   The Te Kooti manhunt was known as *Te Whai a Te Motu* – The Pursuit of the Island.

page 13   "The Powelka Pandemonium" etc. *New Zealand Truth*, 19 April 1910.

page 18   Kimbolton in the 1890s. Stewart Lusk: *Up the Kimbolton Road*, Dunmore Press, Palmerston North, 1988.

page 20   German-speaking immigrants in New Zealand. Gertraut Maria Stoffel: "The Austrian Connection with New Zealand in the Nineteenth Century", in *The German Connection: New Zealand and German-Speaking Europe in the Nineteenth Century*, edited by James N. Bade, Oxford University Press, Auckland, 1993: 21–34.

page 20   "The thing that used to amaze me ...", Jack Hansen interview, Kimbolton, 13 May 1995.

page 21   Grass harvesting. Keith Sinclair and Wendy Harrex: *Looking Back: A Photographic History of New Zealand*, Oxford University Press, Wellington, 1978: 88–92.

page 21   Joe Pawelka's childhood. *New Zealand Times*, 16 April 1910.

page 22   Joe and his father. Jack Harris interview, Kimbolton, 13 May 1995.

page 23   James K. Baxter: "Notes on the Education of a New Zealand Poet", in *The Man on the Horse*, University of Otago Press, Dunedin, 1967: 121.

page 24	Joe Pawelka's letter home. In private hands.
page 28	Background to the Polish emigration to New Zealand. *Polish Settlers in Taranaki 1876–1976*, by Jerzy Woodzimierz Pobog-Jaworowski, Wellington, 1976: 3–4.
page 36	'To Speak of the Woe that is in Marriage' is the title of a poem by Robert Lowell, first published in *Life Studies*.
page 42	The Pawelka legend. The principal source is Albert William Organ's *The True Life Story of Joseph John Pawelka: His Crimes, Sentences, Prison Career, and Final Escape*, Books and Papers, Ltd, Wellington and Auckland, 1912. "Pawelka, the Gaol Breaker", in *The Kaiwarra Mystery ... and More Famous Trials*, by W.H. Carson and Jack R. Sheehan (National Magazines, Wellington, 1935: 17–26) contains no new material. Des Swain's *Pawelka* (Moana Press, Tauranga, 1989) is the first account of Pawelka's life to draw on interviews with the Pawelka family, as well as independent and extensive archival research.
page 45	*The Encyclopaedia of New Zealand* (1966: vol. 2, p. 395) claims that "the origin of the name Manawatu is obscure." The Rangitane mythology is spelled out in J.M. McEwen's *Rangitane: A Tribal History*. Heinemann Reed, Auckland, 1986: 16–17. For other details I am indebted to the late Te Pakaka Tawhai. Personal communication, 29 June 1984.
page 46	"The Black Hole of Calcutta". Editorial in *The Manawatu Evening Standard*, 3 May 1910.
page 49	*In Fires of No Return* is the title of a collection of poems by James K. Baxter, Oxford University Press, London and Wellington, 1958.
page 49	Palmerston North in 1910. George Conrad Petersen: *Palmerston North: A Centennial History*, A.H. & A.W. Reed, Wellington, 1973.
page 53	Swaggers in the Manawatu. George Conrad Petersen: *Palmerston North: A Centennial History*, p. 143. See also John A. Lee: *Roughnecks, Rolling Stones & Rouseabouts*, Whitcoulls, Christchurch, 1977. On footloose young men as scapegoats, see Erik Olssen: "Towards a New Society", in *The Oxford History of New Zealand*,

edited by Geoffrey W. Rice, Oxford University Press, Auckland, 1992: 261.

page 57 Mikal Gilmore: *A Shot in the Heart*, Doubleday, New York 1994: 86, 129, 133–134.

page 61 Pawelka as bogeyman. Many older informants recalled how, when they were children, their parents warned them that Joe Pawelka would 'get them' if they did not behave. According to Judith Binney, an earlier generation used Te Kooti in exactly the same way (*Redemption Songs: a Life of Te Kooti Arikirangi Te Turuki*, Auckland University Press and Bridget Williams Books 1995: 4).

page 66 Stanley Liddicoat's name is given as Lidichen and Linton in other reports. Such journalistic imprecision is typical of both names and dates in newspaper articles covering the Pawelka story. In *The Manawatu Evening Standard*, 29 April 1910, the date of the theft of a steel from Dixon's butchery is given as 13 July 1909; in the *Records of the Magistrates Court* it is given as 6 July. While the *Standard* reports the theft of Ira Gordon's bicycle to have occurred on 9 October 1909, the *Records of the Court* state 1 November.

page 66 Joe Pawelka's note. *Evening Post*, 27 May 1910.

page 67 Pat Hanlon. One may suppose that Hanlon's intolerance of Joe Pawelka's failings reflected the self-congratulatory, vulnerable pride of the self-made man. Starting life as an Irish farm labourer, Hanlon emigrated to New Zealand in 1879 at age 20. He married Lizzie Wilson's elder sister Jinny in 1883 and established himself as carrier and entrepreneur. He owned 'fine stables', the only hearse in the Ashhurst district, and the local coach. According to *The Cyclopaedia of New Zealand* (1897: 208), his business was 'about the best in the district'.

page 72 Joe Pawelka's alibi. Report by Sergeant Bowden, Feilding, 11 October 1911. P1 1910/610 National Archives, Wellington.

page 92 Trade Unions and class divisions in New Zealand circa 1910. I have made use of the following books: Laurie Barber's *New*

Zealand: A Short History, Hutchinson, London, 1990: 87–99; Erik Olssen's "Towards a New Society", in *The Oxford History of New Zealand*, edited by Geoffrey W. Rice, Oxford University Press, Auckland, 1992: 254–284; Miles Fairburn's *The Ideal Society and its Enemies: The Foundations of Modern New Zealand Society 1850–1900*, Auckland University Press, 1989; Tony Simpson's *A Vision Betrayed: The Decline of Democracy in New Zealand*, Hodder and Stoughton, Auckland, 1984.

page 94   'We are not lumps of clay ...' Jean-Paul Sartre: *Saint-Genet* (translated by B. Frechtman), George Braziller, New York, 1963: 49.

page 100   'Indeed, it seems ...' Albert William Organ: *The True Life Story of Joseph John Pawelka*, Books and Papers, Ltd, Wellington, 1912: 75–76. The account of Pawelka's escape attempts is drawn from the Police File (JPD 1911/15/2) which contains a detailed Department of Justice report on both the 17 August attempted escape and the 27 August escape.

page 117   Ray Carter: *Beyond the Call of Duty: A History of the Palmerston North Police District*, Stylex Print, Palmerston North, 1988.

page 125   Sergeant Bowden's report. Feilding, 11 October 1911. P1 1910/610 National Archives, Wellington.

page 126   Constable Fitzgibbon's report. Kimbolton, 28 October 1911. P1 1910/610 National Archives, Wellington.

page 126   Willie Hansen's derogatory remarks. *The Manawatu Evening Standard*, 14 April 1910.

page 133   Butch Cassidy. Quotes from Lula Parker-Betenson's *Butch Cassidy, My Brother* (as told to Dora Flack), Penguin Books, 1976: p. 1, p. 164, p. 168. For details of the Butch Cassidy story see also: Larry Pointer: *In Search of Butch Cassidy*, University of Oklahoma Press, Norman, 1977.

page 133   Review of Robyn Jensen's *Kirsa: A Mother's Story*. 'The Girl Who Never Came Home: A Mother's Agony', *The New Zealand Herald*, Weekend Magazine, 20 August 1994.

page 146   Pawelka at Gallipoli. I am grateful to Des Hurley for bringing to my attention an item which appeared in several New Zealand dailies in February 1916. On the strength of a letter from a soldier who reported seeing Pawelka in the Dardanelles, it was concluded that this must have been Joe. This was probably either wishful thinking or journalistic opportunism. Surely Joe's brother Jack, who was at Gallipoli before being invalided to England with enteric fever, would have heard if his older brother was also there? Although I suppose there is a remote possibility that Jack left the Dardanelles well before the evacuation on 20 December 1915, and that his brother Joe appeared later on the scene, to be spotted by an old mate and made the subject of comment in a letter written between September and December 1915.

page 146   New Zealanders in World War I. *An Encylopaedia of New Zealand*, R.E. Owen, Wellington, vol. 3, 1966: 559–568.

page 149   Pawelka's possible alias. I have checked 25 of the 42 John Wilsons who served in the Australian armed forces in World War I, as well as one Joseph Wilson (d. Auburn NSW 1934, aged 39). I have also checked all but one of the Joseph Wilsons (whose fathers' names were also Joseph) in the NSW Registry of Deaths. I have also checked the New Zealand War Register (1914–1918), but to no avail. As a footnote to this research, Joe Pawelka's cousin and namesake, Joseph Pavelka, was killed accidentally at White Rock in December 1912 – the same year Joe left New Zealand – and another of Joe's cousins, Edward Pavelka, was killed in action in France in June 1916.

page 161   The sale of the section at Edwards Street. 'Pawelka's Flight: Sensational Happenings Recalled by Land Sale', *The Manawatu Evening Standard*, 13 January 1965.

page 176   Aggression and narcissism. See Erich Fromm's *The Anatomy of Human Destructiveness*, Jonathan Cape, London, 1974: 200–205. But of such clinical profiles, Oliver Sacks cautions: 'The danger is that we may go overboard in medicalizing our predecessors (and contemporaries), reducing their complexity to expressions of neurological or psychiatric disorder, while neglecting all the other factors that determine a life, not least the irreducible uniqueness of the individual.' *An Anthropologist on Mars*, Knopf, New York 1995: 165.

page 178   Des Swain's *Pawelka*, Moana Press, Tauranga 1989: 109, 110.

page 179   John Berger's 'The Secretary of Death', in *The Sense of Sight: Writings by John Berger*, Pantheon, New York, 1985: 239–242.

page 181   George Santayana, *The Life of Reason*, 1905: vol. 1, ch. 12.

※